QUITA'S DAY SCARE CENTER 2

A NOVEL BY

GINA

PUBLISHER'S NOTE:
This book is a work of fiction. Names, characters, businesses,
Organizations, places, events and incidents are the product of the
Author's imagination or are used fictionally. Any resemblance of
Actual persons, living or dead, events, or locales are entirely
coincidental.

Library of Congress Control Number: 2012954633
ISBN 10: 0984993037

ISBN 13: 978-0984993031

Cover Design: Davida Baldwin www.oddballdsgn.com
Editor: Advanced Editorial Services
Graphics: Davida Baldwin
www.thecartelpublications.com
First Edition

Printed in the United States of America

CHECK OUT OTHER TITLES BY THE CARTEL PUBLICATIONS

SHYT LIST 1
SHYT LIST 2
SHYT LIST 3
SHYT LIST 4
SHYT LIST 5
PITBULLS IN A SKIRT 1
PITBULLS IN A SKIRT 2
PITBULLS IN A SKIRT 3
POISON 1
POISON 2
VICTORIA'S SECRET
HELL RAZOR HONEYS 1
HELL RAZOR HONEYS 2
BLACK AND UGLY AS EVER
A HUSTLER'S SON 2
THE FACE THAT LAUNCHED A THOUSAND BULLETS
YEAR OF THE CRACKMOM
THE UNUSUAL SUSPECTS
MISS WAYNE AND THE QUEENS OF DC
LA FAMILIA DIVIDED
RAUNCHY
RAUNCHY 2: MAD'S LOVE
RAUNCHY 3: JAYDEN'S PASSION
REVERSED
QUITA'S DAYSCARE CENTER
QUITA'S DAYSCARE CENTER 2
DEAD HEADS
THE END. HOW TO WRITE A BESTSELLING NOVEL IN 30 DAYS

What Up Fam,

I'm sitting here drafting my letter to you from the lab where a lot of classics from The Cartel Publications are produced. As I think about what info I wanna tell you, I had to stop and reflect! The Cartel Publications is five years old, and we are truly humbled, and grateful to each and every one of you who have made this possible! We entered the urban fiction literary world as publishers officially in January of 2008.

Now, on the brink of January 2013, and 28 novels later, we still in this strong and committed to bringing you hot shit! With 5 years in the game, 2013 opens the doors to the Cartel Publications branching out into different genres. Although we are growing, and evolving, as everything in time MUST do to survive, we will NEVER leave our roots of urban fiction. Be on the lookout for our latest and greatest publishing venues. We hope you are just as excited about them as we are!

Now, onto the book at hand, "Quita's DayScare Center 2"! This novel was crazy! There is so much stuff poppin' off in this sequel that I'm sure once you start it, you will not look up until the last page, I promise you.

However, before you go, keeping in line with Cartel tradition, where we honor an author whose journey and literary work we admire, we would like to pay tribute to:

Azarel is the author of, "Bruised 1 and 2", "Daddy's House" and "Carbon Copy". Azarel has been penning novels for years and we hope that this trailblazer continues to drop classics for years to come. Make sure you grab her latest novel, "VIP" and support her publishing brand Life Changing Books!

Ok, I'm out; ya'll get into it! You will not be disappointed!

Much Love, Success and Happiness.

Charisse "C. Wash" Washington
Vice President
The Cartel Publications
www.thecartelpublications.com
www.twitter.com/cartelbooks
www.facebook.com/cartelcafeandbooksstore
www.facebook.com/publishercharissewashington
www.twitter.com/CWashVP
Follow us on Instagram @cartelpublications
Follow me on Instagram @publishercwash

Kimi's blood soaked the gray rope being tied around her neck yet she refused to tell the crazed father, her captor, where his son was.

Flex pulled harder on the rope around Kimi's neck, trying to squeeze the truth out of her. He felt like he was in a nightmare. One minute he dropped his son off at Quita's Daycare Center, and the next minute he was coming to pick him up only to learn that Cordon had been kidnapped. Quick investigation on Quita's part led both of them to Kimi, and now Flex wanted answers. He wanted his son.

Quita and Flex watched over Kimi's bloodied body as she lay on the living room floor of Cash's house. In Kimi's crime spree for the day she killed Cash, for raping her months earlier, disposed of his body, and occupied his home as a getaway. But, since Flex found her it was evident that her plan didn't work.

Kimi's beef with Flex ran deep, and she had plans to hurt him both physically and mentally. However, at the moment there was nothing Kimi could do to carry out her full plan. She was badly bruised due to the beating Flex put on her body, which caused her to be unrecognizable. But, revenge did something to her mental state. It made her stronger. It made her bolder.

"Kimi, just tell him where Cordon is, please," Quita said to her. "If you don't he's going to kill you," she continued as she looked down at her.

When Kimi tried to move, Flex stomped on the middle of her back with his shoe. Kimi was on her stomach, with her wrists and ankles tied behind her body. He would tug on the rope, which was wrapped around her neck, ever so often to maintain control.

Where was his son? And, why hadn't he called? Before long Flex remembered. He hated himself for changing his cell number before he could make Cordon memorize it. He'd checked the voicemail at home so many times that his fingers were numb. Through it all, Cordon had not called.

"You not going no where, bitch," Flex said angrily. "Not until you tell me where my son is."

"Please just tell him, Kimi," Quita cried as tears rolled down her face. "He's not playing."

"I don't know what he's talking about," Kimi giggled, as blood poured out of her mouth. "I'm dead already," she looked up at Flex. "Ask him."

"You're not going to kill her right?" Quita questioned Flex.

Silence.

"He's not answering you because I'm dead already. So if he's going to kill me, let's get it on. I'm tired of this world anyway."

He tugged on the rope again and was irritated when he realized he was more out of breath than she was. "Why you doing this shit? I know you know where Cordon is," he wanted her in pain, but not dead. Flex knew that if she died, the location of his son would too. "Tell me where Cordon is! I promise I'll let you go, just as long as he's safe."

Kimi laughed, "Sorry, Flex. I don't know anything."

Quita felt both anger and sorrow for her friend. Mainly because Quita couldn't understand how she got tied up into Kimi's drama. Things that day started out average but turned to watery shit quick. And it started with Kimi's cousin and Quita's former assistant, Pooh.

EARLIER THAT DAY

Quita gave Pooh the van to take Joshua, Zaboy, and Cordon to the movies. She was taking care of business, when the next thing she knew, she got word that Pooh was being arrested for driving erratically and without a valid driver's license. One thing led to Pooh fainting in the officer's arms without telling him where to take the kids. Pooh could've gotten arrested and the parents would've gone ballistic on her. However, it was Cordon who thought quickly on his feet and memorized Quita's information to give the officers.

The officers bought the children home, and the first thing she did was fire Pooh.

Quita was so proud of Cordon that she decided to call Vonzella, one of the parents of the kids she watched named Miranda. Miranda hadn't been to her daycare center ever since Quita questioned Vonzella about the men around her daughter. In retaliation, Vonzella pulled Miranda out of her center, breaking Cordon's heart in the process.

Quita was quite all right with not kissing Vonzella's ass or seeing her daughter again. But, she knew Cordon didn't feel the same, and she wanted to reward him for his quick thinking with the cops. Quita rewarded Cordon by sucking up to a bitch that she thought was nothing more than a worthless mother. In the end, her plan worked because she was able to bring Miranda over to surprise Cordon.

Things were cool as she watched Cordon, Miranda, Zaboy and Joshua enjoy chocolate ice cream at her kitchen table. Ten minutes into the fun, the usual occurred when Joshua shat all over himself. She took him to the bathroom to clean him up. But, instead of just cleaning him up and changing his clothes, she was in for a shocker. She learned that he was being raped because his little body was covered in bites and his underpants had blood in the seat.

Taking Joshua to get medical attention, she left the other children in her assistant Essence's care as she took Joshua to the hospital. She also called her on again and off again boyfriend Demetrius, to give Essence some help with the children.

When Quita got to the hospital, she learned that Joshua's real name was Joey Kennan and that he had been abducted from his home in Houston Texas years ago. His abductor was none other than Wondrika, his fake mother, who was really a man. Wondrika's birth name was actually Wallace George, and he was a convicted pedophile who was wanted by law enforcement.

Quita experienced so many emotions, that all she wanted to do was go home and gather herself.

Although Quita was pleased that she was able to assist Joshua in being reunited with his family, when she returned home, she found that her world had been turned upside down. Her daycare center was empty. Although most of the kids had been reunited with their families, Cordon was missing and Flex wanted answers.

In Quita's plight to help Flex, she learned that many stories were going on right up under her nose. For starters, she discovered that her long time friend Valencia Malone, along with Valencia's ex-boyfriend Tech, planned to kidnap Flex's father for ransom.

When the ransom call came in, Tech failed to say whom he had in his possession. Flex assumed it was Cordon, since he was missing. Flex threatened Valencia, and to save her own head, Valencia gave them Tech's address. But, when they went to Tech's home, they discovered that the kidnapping they planned included Flex's father, not his son. This confused and frustrated Flex even more.

Flex wasn't interested in saving his father. He had beef with his father, after discovering that he raped his wife. So needless to say he could care less what they did to him.

Flex was about to light the house on fire until Quita told him she had an idea, but that she needed to go alone to check her lead. Flex agreed, but secretly followed Quita anyway. It was then that he discovered that the trip led him to Kimi, the biological mother of his son, Cordon. Flex was rocked because he had no idea that Kimi was aware of his deceit. And, that he was raising their son, whom he told her was dead.

Quita observed Flex pull tighter on the rope. "You're going to kill her," she told him softly. "And then you'll never find out where Cordon is."

Flex stopped what he was doing and rushed toward Quita. "Do you know where my son is, bitch? You was in here forever before Morton and me got here. How I know you don't have something to do with all of this shit?"

Quita's large framed backed up into the couch and she toppled over. She tried to scramble to her feet but Flex was already hanging over her. His neat cornrows were glistening from sweat, and strands of hair unraveled from the rows, and drew up into curls surrounding his face.

Quita knew he was angry, and she had to be careful with what she said to him. "Flex, I love—"

Flex slapped her so hard her face went numb. "Don't tell me you love my son!" Flex pointed in her face. "Don't ever tell me you love him again! I'm the only one alive who gives a fuck about him!"

"I didn't mean it like that, Flex. It's just that, I really like the kid. Even with you killing my mother tonight because you thought I was involved, I still wanted to help you. You're not the only person who has lost someone they loved."

Earlier that day, when Cordon went missing from Quita's daycare center, Flex said something to Quita that rocked her heart. *"I hope you said goodbye to your mother."*

Quita knew then that she would never see her mother alive again. When she went to the nursing home to check on her, just like she thought, she was dead.

It wasn't like Quita didn't know that Flex was capable of violence. When he dropped Cordon off to her daycare the first time, he made himself clear. His exact words were, *'If one hair is harmed on his head, it won't be good for you. So think clearly before taking my paper.'*

All Quita could think about was the three thousand dollars a week she was going to get for watching Cordon. Greed hid her from seeing what Flex really meant. She had one job, and it was to make sure Cordon was okay. Yet she failed.

"I killed your mother because you failed to protect my son. But I'm going to kill more than her if Cordon isn't found." Flex promised.

"You mean, my son." Kimi said, as blood continued to ooze out of her mouth.

Flex moved toward Kimi. Standing over top of Kimi Flex responded, "I meant exactly what I said. He's my son."

"I loved you, Thomas," she laughed, "Or is it Flex?" She paused. "Seven years ago you were the light of my life. I would've given anything to be with you and still you wanted more."

"You don't even know what you're talking about," he said under his breath. "I didn't make you do anything you didn't want to."

"I was such a fool. So dumb for letting you convince me that I didn't want to be a mother. That I didn't want my only child. That my son was actually dead!"

"You gave him up on your own, Kimi. I didn't twist your arm. I didn't put a gun to your head. All you had to do was fight for him."

Kimi gave him a look so evil; he buckled a little. This was major because even though she was tied up, Kimi was the scariest person in the room. "I remember everything about that day. Everything."

SEVEN YEARS AGO

The movie theater was filled to capacity, as Kimi sat in the back of the theater with her long-term boyfriend Thomas. Softly nudging him on the arm she whispered, "Hey, baby. I'm going to the bathroom. I'll be right back. You want something?" She felt like she had to take a serious dump, that couldn't wait until she got home.

"Huh?" He whispered, never taking his eyes off of the screen. The movie was on the best part. "Why you talking in the theater? You know how much I hate that shit."

"I'm sorry. I just..." she stopped before completing her sentence because she realized he probably wouldn't care anyway. "Nevermind."

"When you come back bring me a small popcorn...extra butter," he said as he continued watching the movie screen. "And a soda too."

"Where's the money?"

"Girl, get out of my face and go get my shit."

"Yeah whatever, Thomas." As she made her way carefully down the steps in the theater, she focused on the exit. Her pregnant belly made it difficult to walk. Ever since she discovered she was pregnant, Thomas rejected and neglected her. He made it clear that he didn't want the baby, and although her pregnancy came as a result of both of their actions, he didn't hesitate to lay the blame on her shoulders.

Easing past the movie watchers, she excused herself and ran down the steps. She couldn't believe how her stomach ached and she was sure if she didn't hurry, she was on the verge of soiling her pants with her own feces. With each step she took, the pain grew more intense, so she darted down the hall, praying she'd make it to the restroom in time.

Flinging the door open, she ran into an empty stall and sat on a toilet, without placing a seat cover on it. Sitting on a toilet, wet with the urine of strangers, she placed her hands on the sides of the stall walls and pushed with all her might. She cried out in agony because she never experienced so much pain in all her life. When she felt her flesh tearing between her legs, she screamed out, "Help me! Please! Somebody help me!"

"Are you alright in there?" Someone asked outside of her stall. "Can I do something for you?"

"Yes, please get me some help and tell my boyfriend I'm in here," Kimi cried. "I think I'm about to have my baby."

"Okay...uh...what's his name? And what theater is he in?" She sounded concerned and Kimi was hopeful she'd help her. "I'll go get him now."

"His name is Thomas and he's in movie theater number 4. Please! Go now!"

The woman scurried away and five minutes later, entered the bathroom with Thomas. He didn't care if it was a woman's bathroom or not, he wanted to know what was going on. For a second he was preparing to pull out his gat, thinking somebody was setting him up, until he saw the blood streaming under the door and heard Kimi wincing in pain. It was then that he knew exactly what was up. She was going into labor in a public place. At that time the plan changed, because all Thomas cared about was getting her out of the ladies room, before people started asking questions.

"I'm coming in, baby," he said softly. "Everything will be alright. Open the door for me." Kimi unlocked the latch and he eased inside. He closed the door and said, "Get up...we got to get out of here." He hoisted her off of the toilet, pulled her panties up, followed by her pants. Blood was over everything...her clothing...his shoes, and his hands. He was focused, and on a mission, and there was nothing anybody could do to stop him. "She'll be alright, I'm taking her to the hospital." He

told concerned by-standers. He didn't take a breath, until they were outside and moving toward his truck. "We almost there. Hold on, baby."

She heard him, but didn't understand why they couldn't wait for the ambulance. The baby wanted out and it wanted out now. But, Thomas wouldn't rest until he had her hidden inside of his Nissan truck. He placed her on the backseat, and she lay out, gripping the bottom of her stomach. "You think you can make it to my apartment, Kimi? I'ma drive fast as shit, so don't worry about that. I just don't want you to push it out while I'm driving."

She raised her head and said, "Your apartment? I need to go to the fuckin' hospital, Thomas! What are you talking about? I'm in pain and am about to have this baby! It can't wait."

"No! That's not how it's going down!" he yelled, placing the car in drive, while looking in the rear view mirror at her frightened face. "If we go there it'll be harder to leave and I can't risk that."

"It'll be harder to leave? Wha...What...What are you talking about?" She asked as the pain continued to rip through her body. She never imagined having a baby would hurt so badly. "I don't want to leave the hospital, I want help."

"We can't keep this baby. I told you that. We agreed on what we were goin' to do remember? So don't back out on me now, Kimi. It's time for you to step up and prove how much you love me. Just as much as I love you."

It's funny how Thomas only told Kimi he loved her when he wanted her to get rid of the baby, after it was too late to get an abortion. "But...it's our baby! I can't do this!" She shook her head. "I can't give our child up! I love him already."

Thomas began to drive erratically and Kimi was thrown around in the truck. He didn't say anything to her until he convinced her that there were now only two choices. Commit to keep the baby and die right now, or give it up for adoption like they discussed. Slowing his pace he said, "It's either me or it. You can't have both of us."

"But why, Thomas?" she cried. "I love my baby already. Don't you? You haven't even seen him yet."

"If you have this baby to spite me, you'll be caring for it alone," Thomas threatened.

Kimi couldn't respond because the baby continued to push its way out of her body. So she rose up, and removed her jeans, followed by her panties. She opened her legs and pushed every time she felt contractions. The back of his truck looked like a crime scene with blood and bodily fluids everywhere. When Thomas realized what was happening, and that she was going to have the baby now, he pulled the truck behind a row of stores and parked. They were surrounded by the night sky and since the stores were closed, it was very private. He got out of the truck and walked to the back of it. He could see the baby's head crown, and all he could think about was getting it over with. "You almost done. Just push for me."

Kimi bit down on her bottom lip so hard, it bled. She placed her hands on each of her knees and screamed out in agony as the baby slid from her body. She pulled him out, and the amniotic sac rested on her stomach. Since he wouldn't cry, she stuck her finger in his mouth to clear his passageway, and hit his bottom.

A smile spread across her face when he wept, and looked into her eyes. He saw her. She knew it.

She laughed at that moment, and looked at Thomas hoping he could love their new baby now, but the look in Thomas' eyes told her he was disconnected from the situation. Thomas took some dirty scissors out of the glove compartment, and snipped the umbilical cord. Removing the baby from her arms, he wrapped him in one of the old jackets in the back of his truck. With the baby still crying, he carefully placed him in the passenger seat next to him.

Although she was in pain Kimi rose up and said, "What you gonna do with him? What you gonna do with my baby?"

"Don't worry about that." He knew that he would have to drop her off first, before he handled his business. "Just lay back and get some rest."

"Thomas, please. Don't do this to me."

He looked at her sternly and said, "Don't make me tell you again, Kimi. I don't wanna hear shit from you or I'll kill you, and this mothafucka! You acting like you didn't know we couldn't keep a kid. Sit the fuck back...and shut the fuck up!"

Kimi layed down and covered her mouth with both of her bloody hands to silence her cries. She couldn't understand how he wasn't even man enough, to consider the baby's safety. He was acting coldly. How could she love him for so long? Now she knew why Thomas didn't want her to go to the hospital. He knew the moment she breastfed the baby, she would never give him up.

Days after the incident, she wondered where her baby was and she watched TV religiously for news of his death. She received the news three days later, when Thomas brought her a newspaper article showing that a baby had been found dead in an abandoned car not too far from where she gave birth. Two days after that...Thomas ended the relationship for good. To think that she gave her baby up, only to be dumped by him, made it difficult for her to live. It was her biggest regret.

Thomas shook his head after hearing her recall true events. He could've lied and said she was wrong, but it would've been for everybody else's sake, and he wasn't in the mood.

"You made your decision on what you wanted to do. You decided to give up your son for me, and when you did that, he became mine. I raised him good and took care of him for seven years."

"You were selfish and cheated Cordon of a full life," Kimi corrected him. "All so you could raise him with another bitch!" She sobbed. "Why?"

"Because Charlene couldn't have kids!" Flex shot back.

"But why take mine?" Tears mixed with blood pushed down her cheeks. "There were plenty of girls who would've had a baby for you."

"Because she wanted my son," he grabbed his dick. "She wanted a kid that had my blood and you already had that."

Kimi's head dropped to the floor and she cried into it. "I feel like such a fucking fool," she said in a muffled voice. "So dumb."

"Kimi, where's my son?"

"I'll never tell you," she said strongly, looking into his eyes. "I'd rather kill him than to see you with him again. He deserves better. Even if it means death."

Although to some it may have seemed as if Kimi was just bitter and angry, Quita knew she was serious about not wanting Cordon to be with Flex. In fact before Flex arrived Kimi said, "If I can't have him, nobody will."

Flex heard a lot of their conversation outside of the door, before he walked inside, but he didn't hear the part about where his son was.

"I'm sick of this shit! If you not gonna tell me where my son is, you're useless to me." Flex raised the gun and was about to shoot her.

Until Quita walked up behind him and said, "I got another idea. Let me make a call, and if it doesn't work, you can do whatever you want to her."

"I'm going to do whatever I want to her anyway," he corrected her.

CHAPTER TWO

The motel room was stuffy because the heat was up way too high. Pooh's googly eyes rolled over young Cordon so many times, as he sat on one of the twin beds, that she was dizzy. She couldn't help herself from looking at him. She was actually staring at who she believed to be her cousin, Kimi's son and she wondered how it was possible. As far as Pooh knew, Kimi didn't have any children and she didn't even like kids. Yet in her opinion, the resemblance he had with Kimi was uncanny.

Although Cordon was in another world, playing with his video game, Miranda was sitting directly next to Cordon and staring into Pooh's pink lips as she spoke on the phone. If Pooh weren't so nervous about Cordon, she would've taken notice that she was the object of the little girl's eye.

Pooh's cell phone was pressed so hard against her lips that they were bleeding. "I can't believe it, Davie," she whispered. "Cordon is Kimi's son. I'm telling you he's her son. But, what I want to know is what is she doing with him? I think she's going to hurt him or something because she would've told me she had him."

"Stop that wild talking," Davie said. " You don't know if he's her kid or not," he burped. "You always making things out to be more than what they is. Did you try calling her back again?"

"I did, but she's not answering the phone."

"Relax, Pooh. And just wait to hear from Kimi. She gonna sort it all out."

"I don't care what you say, I know my family when I see them," Pooh sighed looking at Cordon. "He's related to us. I just can't believe I waited so long to notice. It's not like I haven't been around this kid before. I use to watch him at Quita's daycare center and I never noticed. I got a bad feeling something is going to happen to these kids."

When she finally saw Miranda eavesdropping she said, "Hold on, Davie." She put her phone down and glared back at Miranda. "What the fuck you doing listening to my personal conversations? Huh?"

Scared, Miranda shrugged and said, "I'm thirsty." The light in the room bounced off of her shiny black ponytail and her light skin turned pink. "I didn't mean to be listening."

"Bitch, I done told you I'm on the phone right now, at least five times," Pooh continued, laying into the little girl. "I'll take you to get a soda later."

Cordon immediately stopped what he was doing and his eyes rested on Pooh's pointy nose. "Ms. Pooh, can you not talk to her like that again?" He asked with respect. "It's not nice and I don't like it."

Pooh's frown disintegrated and she smiled at the cute boy. Although Cordon got one out on her, by putting her in her place, she was proud that he stepped up for his girlfriend. It meant he wasn't a punk.

"I'm sorry, Cordon," she tried to smile but she wasn't a Miranda fan. "I'm just busy right now, why don't ya'll go get the soda yourself. It's outside down the hall. You said you got money right?"

"Yes," he told her.

"Okay, well go get one for her and come right back."

Cordon put his video game down and walked toward the door with Miranda on his heels. When they were in the hallway they underestimated how cold they would be without their coats.

"Hold up, I gotta go back and get my money," Cordon said.

"Now," Miranda grabbed his soft hand and pulled him closer. "You can't go back inside."

A lady with long brown braids passed them in the hallway and said, "How cute! You two are so adorable."

"Thank you, ma'am," Cordon said looking at the floor. "I appreciate the compliment."

"Oh my God!" she placed her hand over her heart. "And you have manners," she cooed. "Not sure who your parents are but I'll say this, they've done a good job with you." The lady left them alone and disappeared into a door that said office on the outside.

When she was gone Miranda whispered, "Cordon, who is your mommy?"

"What you mean?" He frowned stepping away from her. "My mother's name is Charlene."

Cordon liked Miranda but he didn't like talking about his mother. It was a sore spot for him. Mainly because Charlene took her own life for reasons he couldn't understand. Why didn't she want to be his mother? Didn't she realize where he would be in the world without her?

Part of Cordon hated Charlene, and the other part remembered the good times they shared before she put a gun to her head, and pulled the trigger. Like when she would walk into his room, and kiss him before volunteering at the church everyday. If he were up when she came inside his room, he'd act like he was too big for the nonsense. But what he wouldn't give to have that moment now.

"I know, and I'm not trying to make you mad and stuff. I just heard something and I wanted to see if it was true."

"Well, what you hear?"

"Ms. Pooh said your mother is Kimi. The lady that use to watch us before you got there."

"I remember her," he said. "She came to pick me up, from some strange man's house earlier today."

"What you mean?"

"Quita's boyfriend took me from the daycare center to his house. A little while later, Kimi came over and took me out of his house. The next thing I know, Pooh has me and they went to get you." Cordon seemed more confused now.

"I think…I think…" Miranda stuttered. For some reason, she couldn't bring herself to tell him what she overheard about Kimi being his mother. What if it was a lie? What if she was wrong?

"What you about to say, Miranda?"

She reddened. "I…I…think…"

"Are you okay," he asked holding her hand.

"I don't trust Ms. Pooh," she said softly. "She seems creepy to me and I want to leave."

He laughed. "Pooh loud sometimes, but she seems okay to me."

"That's cause she's always nice to you." Miranda felt a tinge of jealousy. "What you like her or something?"

He laughed again. "Naw, I don't like her," he squeezed her hand. "The only girl I like is you."

Miranda blushed and pawed the locket he bought for her that hung around her neck. He gave it to her. She cherished the gift because the first boy she'd ever liked gave it to her, and it had a picture of a piano inside of it. She played whenever she was at school and he remembered.

"I know you like me, boy," she said pushing him back.

He grinned. "Then what's wrong?"

"I'm serious, I don't know about Ms. Pooh." She brushed her hair out of her face. "She seemed real creepy when she was on the phone. I think she was talking to her boyfriend."

"What did you hear her say?"

"When you were playing on the video game, I think she said she thinks something bad is going to happen to us."

His eyebrows rose. "So what you want to do about it?" He asked seriously.

"I think if we stay, something bad is going to happen like she said. Maybe we should just leave."

He shook his head. "And go where? We just kids."

"Yeah, but I don't want to be a dead one. Do you?" When he didn't seem to be responding she said, "Please let's go, Cordon. I don't want to go back in there."

"What about our coats? And I have my money in there too."

"If we get our coats she might not let us leave again," she said softly looking toward the door. "We gotta go now."

Cordon saw the fear in her eyes. No he didn't want to leave Pooh, and risk getting lost outside in the world. But he wanted to be a man, the kind he saw his father be. He decided leaving with her, and making sure she was okay, was better than nothing at all.

"If we gonna leave, we gotta get help," Cordon said seriously. "So follow me."

CHAPTER THREE

As Valencia sat on the floor inside of Tech's house, she stared at the phone on the kitchen wall so long, her eyes dried out. To make shit worse, her back was leaning against the couch and the bones in her ass ached. One minute she was plotting a kidnapping, and the next minute she was waiting for the call that could end her life. She prayed it wouldn't come.

Flex's father creepily looking at her, across the living room, also made her uncomfortable. Every time Leroy stared in her direction, he was looking between her legs at her fat pussy lips print that popped out in her jeans. Leroy had his arms tied behind his back, as he leaned up against the wall.

When Valencia looked to her left, her boyfriend Tech was lying on the floor, soaking it with his blood. Earlier that evening Flex's goon, Maine, shot Tech in the leg when they first entered the house, believing he had his son instead of his father Leroy. The shit blew up in their faces when Flex revealed he could give a fuck about his father.

Still, as Valencia eyeballed Tech, he looked so pathetic that she felt sorry for him.

"How you feel, baby?" She whispered, not knowing where Maine was in the house. Flex had Maine hang back until he pursued the lead Quita had on his son. "You still in pain?"

"What you think, bitch?" Tech shouted. "You got me in this shit and now these niggas gonna kill me," he tried to move his leg, "if I don't bleed to death first. So to answer your question, yes, I'm in a lot of got damn pain!"

Valencia frowned, and her heart ached. "If I recall, you were the one who ate my pussy and convinced me to do this ransom shit, Tech. I didn't want to be bothered, remember? But, to please you I went against my conscious. So don't try to put this shit on me."

"Fuck," Tech yelled as the pain from the bullet wound intensified. "I need to see a doctor!" He called out into the house, ignoring Valencia. "Do you hear me, mothafucka? I need a doctor or some medicine! I'm dying out here!"

Maine flew out of the back room with an attitude. His six-foot four-inch heavy frame was intimidating. "The only thing you gonna get is another bullet if you don't shut the fuck up!"

When Tech smelled the weed streaming around him he said, "So what, you smoking up my shit now? What part of the game is that?"

"You lost the rights to all your shit when you fucked with Flex. Now shut the fuck up before I put you out of your misery making pain the last thing on your mind," Maine laughed and moseyed to the back of the house.

"I hate these mothafuckas," Tech whispered. "If I get out of here, on everything I love, I'm gonna kill these mothafuckas one by one. Starting with Flex and ending at that fat ass mothafucka back there. That's on the President! I'm not even fucking around with them."

While Tech promised to annihilate everyone, Valencia peeped over at Leroy again. She feared Leroy would tell Flex what Tech said, until she remembered he was in the same predicament. If Flex gave a fuck about him, Leroy wouldn't be in there.

As if he could read her mind Leroy said, "Close your stinking legs. Don't nobody want to smell that shit."

"I don't know what you smell over there, but over here, the air couldn't be fresher," Valencia responded.

Leroy tried to sit up but the awkward position his hands were tied in, behind his back, forced him to lay sideways against the wall. "Well don't nobody want to see all that shit either."

She crossed her legs and frowned. "Then why you looking?" She was disgusted by him, especially after learning that he raped his own daughter-in-law, impregnated her, and gave her HIV. In her opinion, Flex was better off in the world without a father like him.

"You's an old smart mouth bitch ain't you?" He laughed. "You have no idea of what I would do with bitches like you. Be lucky you over there and I'm over here. For now anyway."

"I should've stayed with Brooke," Tech said out of left field. He was referring to his ex-girlfriend. "I knew the moment I saw her in high school, that she was the one for me. " He looked at Valencia and sweat poured down his face. "If I make it out of here alive, we through. I don't want to see you or talk to you ever again. Are we clear on that shit?"

"I really can't believe you're blaming me for this." She couldn't lie, although he was far from the man of her dreams at the moment, his words stung. Down deep. "The last thing we need to be doing right now is going against each other. If we gonna get out of this alive, we have to put our heads together."

Across the room Leroy moaned, and sat up straight to look down the hallway in Maine's direction. When no one was coming he leaned back. "There's a knife downstairs," he said softly.

"And just what the fuck are we supposed to do with that?" Tech asked. "In case you haven't noticed, we not in the position right now to do shit, main man. We don't have the use of our hands."

"That's you young people of today's problem," he said sucking his teeth. "You don't see the possibilities even when they right in front of you."

"And what possibilities do we have right now?" Valencia inquired. "Enlighten us. I want to know."

"We can get out of here," Leroy continued whispering in their direction. "We don't have to leave it to this fool to pull the trigger or not. Our destiny is in our own hands," he preached, trying to sit up straight again before rolling back on his side. "It's time we put our heads together, and come up with a plan for escape. I want that mothafucka back there dead. He's feeling himself too much for me."

"To be honest, I don't think he's the person we have to worry about," Tech said to Leroy. "Your son is."

Leroy laughed heartedly. Realizing he may have been a little too loud, he rolled over on his stomach and looked back into the hallway. No one was coming. So Leroy said, "Let me tell you something, young, man. My son won't do anything to harm me so I'm not even worried about that."

Valencia eyed the rope that was tied so tightly around Leroy's wrist, that some of his chocolate skin had rubbed off, revealing a pink center. If anything he was in the same boat they were, even if he didn't know it. "You do realize you're hemmed up just like us don't you?" She asked him. "If your son wanted you free he would've released you."

Leroy looked at her. "Let me tell you something about my son. He is a family man. Always has been. Did you see the look in his eyes when he walked in this fucking apartment, and saw that dick wad over there had me tied up like some sort of pig?" He waited for confirmation but no one said a mumbling word.

In Valencia's opinion Leroy was delusional and ridiculous. "Leroy, I think you are way off about how things went down here tonight."

"I'm right in the mind, you just worry about yourself. My baby boy would've lit this place on fire if I was dead. Like I was telling, you, my boy's a family man and he wouldn't hurt me."

Maine walked back into the living room and said, "What the fuck are ya'll whispering about out here?" His eyes were as red as raspberries and clouds of smoke hovered over his head as he waited for an answer. The large dick bulge in his jeans disgusted her because she hated for monsters to be packing. "The only thing you niggas need to be in here talking about is Flex's kid, and if you know where he is or not."

Although Maine was chilling in the backroom, he wasn't worried about them escaping. Fortunately for Maine, Tech had a front door, which locked, from the inside and he had the only key. Not to mention he had them tied up really good by their wrists and ankles.

"We good out here," Leroy said, trying to take control over the situation. "And, ain't no need in you worrying about what we talking about. Just 'cause you have us tied up, don't mean we not grown, and can't have a private conversation."

For Leroy's snide comment, Maine sent a boot to his chin, sending him flying upward and against the wall. He was finally in the position he'd been trying to get into all day. The fucked up part was, his physical condition had changed.

Blood poured out of his mouth like a water fountain, and drenched his shirt. And in case he thought no real damage had been done, two of his teeth unloaded themselves from his mouth, and lie next to him like two dice.

"Shut the fuck up, nigga," Maine told Leroy. "Matta of fact, I don't want you saying shit to me period."

Leroy sucked up his blood and said, "My son gonna get you for that shit." His words whistled through his teeth and landed on deaf ears. "I hope you ready for what's gonna happen."

"If only you knew the real deal," Maine shook his head. "Trust me man, you ain't in no position to do shit but die." He looked at Valencia and Tech and said, "Now everybody shut the fuck up, before I give you all free dental work." He strutted back to Tech's room and slammed the door.

"On second thought I was wrong," Tech said in a sarcastic weak voice. "You do got a lot of pull around here. You had the nigga practically falling at your feet."

"Harder than the president of the united states," Valencia whispered trying not to laugh loudly.

Leroy was so angry and embarrassed he was trembling. "If ya'll would clean the nut out of your ears, you'd hear what I been trying to say all day."

Valencia's eyes popped open at his weird comment.

"It ain't about Maine," Leroy continued pointing in Maine's direction. "He in here showboating and would never listen to reason. Us getting out of here is about my son. Trust me, Flex not going to kill me and if you help me get out, I can convince him not to kill you too."

Valencia was bored and scared so she decided to humor him. Besides, what did she have to lose?" What's your plan?"

He leaned toward them and whispered lower, "Like I was trying to say earlier, there is a knife downstairs in the basement. It's under the recliner. I was using it earlier to cut these ropes when your little boyfriend had me downstairs. If we can get to it, and cut ourselves out, we as good as gold."

"I knew you didn't have shit worthwhile to say." Tech said, closing his eyes. "Just leave me alone. I want to die in peace."

"Why not go in the kitchen and get a knife?" Valencia inquired.

"Because the nigga Maine took all of the knives in the room," Leroy responded.

Valencia remembered where Tech kept his specialty knives. Deep in the back of the top shelves. She wondered if Maine took them too. She would only move on that jewel when she could. Now was not the time.

"So what are you going to do?" Valencia asked. "Crawl downstairs or something? Because the moment you do, he's going to come outside of that room and stomp you into the floorboard. You felt what he just did to you." She observed his bloody mess. "You want another dose of that shit?"

"I didn't feel a thing."

"Then you really are crazy," Valencia said, leaning back into the seat. She was finally convinced that nothing good could come from talking to the man. "Just leave me alone."

"I haven't told you my plan."

"You haven't said shit yet."

"Well I'm ready to tell you how we can get out of this situation. My only question is, are you listening or not?"

Silence.

"Well?" He continued frustrated at her lack of response.

"Whatever you want to share, just say it. To be honest, I'm getting very bored with you."

"We get out of here, by you seducing Maine," Leroy smiled. "Don't you see, he was looking at you from the moment you got in here. It's clear where his mind is at. He wants to fuck! If you say the right things we can be free."

Valencia was hopeful until she learned that their plan for freedom entailed her. "I'm not a whore."

"Stop lying to yourself, Valencia," Tech said back in the conversation. "Because as much as I hate to believe it, the old man has a point. He's back there getting high, and you and me both know what comes after that. Food and sex. It's the perfect time."

Valencia hated everyone in the room. For as angry as she was, she also knew they were right. Not only had Maine been trying to fuck her since he was at her house earlier, drinking up all of her beer, and smoking up all of her weed, she sincerely may have been their only hope. But doubt was heavy over her.

"I don't know about this," She said in a low voice.

"Then you must be ready to die," Tech said, softly. "And you must be ready for me to die too." When he saw he was getting to her he became Babe Ruth and started knocking it out of the park. "You are good at this shit, baby. You can get this nigga to do anything you want."

Suddenly her heart felt warm again for him. Tech always knew the right things to say. And, perhaps this was all her fault. She started retracing her part in the ransom plan again. She should've never given Flex Tech's address when he held the gun to her head at her house. She should've taken that bullet and waited for him in the next life.

With her breasts poked out and her chin held high, she decided to ride and slide for her man. "Okay, I'll do it."

Both Leroy and Tech smiled wider than the Brooklyn Bridge. They both worked her over and if she played it up right, they would be out of there within the hour.

Valencia looked in the direction Maine went in. She took a deep breath, licked her lips and called his name.

Pooh looked some kind of stupid, siting on the edge of the bed trembling. She lost both Cordon and Miranda and knew she could officially say goodbye to her black ass. Because once Kimi found out, she was going to tear into her. That's if Flex didn't kill her first.

Pooh had seen Kimi lose it when she didn't get her way. When Pooh use to go over Kimi's house as a child, so Kimi could babysit her, Pooh never got into trouble because Kimi threatened her into submission. To prove her meanness, and that she meant business, Kimi popped the heads off of all of Pooh's doll baby's, and broke her pet bird's neck. As if that weren't enough, Kim then boiled the deceased fowl in a large silver pot on the stove. Kimi made it clear that she planned to do the same things to Pooh if she got on her bad side, and Pooh feared that the moment finally arrived.

After looking for Cordon and Miranda for an hour with no luck, she decided it was best for her to come back into the room and stare at the walls. Perhaps if she looked at them hard enough, they would reveal their exact location like a GPS system. Two hours later, even the walls let her down.

Pooh leaped up, and decided to call the motel personnel. Maybe they were somewhere sitting in the office waiting on her to pick them up. When she called zero to get the operator, and assumed it was a white person on the other line, she tried to put on her most professional voice. "Uhmm, yes, I'm calling to see if my kids is there?"

"I don't understand," said the receptionist.

Frustrated that the woman didn't understand her dumb ass question she got louder, thinking this would do the trick. "Is my kids down there or not? That's what I'm calling to see."

"Ma'am, we don't have any children down here. Are you sure you called the right—"

"Then you should've said that, you monkey face, bitch!" Having set the woman straight who she had never seen before, she paced the room. "Kimi's going to kill me. I don't want to die. Please God don't let her kill me."

When the wheels in her brain started to squeak, she decided to call her boyfriend. Sure he was twenty-five years old with a fifth grade education. And, yes he often got lost walking around his own neighborhood. But, he was her Barack and she was his Michelle and their dysfunctions were nobody's business.

"Davie, I think I fucked up some kind of good," she said with the phone pressed against her ear. "I need you bad right now because I'm so scared. This is worse than anything I may have done before."

"Hold on, mama," he told her. "I'm trying to put this last coat of clear polish on my toenails." He sat the phone down and she heard it clank.

His response was wrong on many levels. First off he was a grown ass man, second it was cold outside and as far as she knew, his feet wouldn't be showing. And, last but not least, she needed his help. It took Davie three minutes to return to the phone and she hung on for every last minute.

"Now what's up with my baby?" Davie questioned.

"I lost, Miranda and Cordon," she cried as her salt water fell into her mouth. "Kimi is going to let lose on me when she find out. And I don't even know what Cordon's father might do. Or Miranda's mother. I was supposed to be watching that little girl to keep Cordon company."

"First off, Kimi is a human being like you and me. She got a nose, eyes and ears. So what do we care?"

Pooh was totally confused. I mean, what the fuck was he talking about? She often told him dipping his cigarettes with Embalming fluid wasn't the move, and now it was coming back to haunt him.

"Davie, I need you to come pick me up from the motel. I know you had plans to see your grandmother in the hospital, but this more important than anything. Please."

Silence.

When she hadn't gotten a response, she looked at the phone to be sure it was still on. When it was, she placed her head to the set and said, "Davie…are you still there? I need you to come get me."

"I'm sorry, baby. I forgot what we were talking about. What's going on again?"

She sighed but used his lapse in memory to her advantage. "You said you were on your way to pick me up. You need the address again?"

"Naw, I think I'll remember it. I'll be there in five minutes."

"You gotta come now, Davie. This is serious. Don't wait five minutes or an hour. Come now."

****

An hour later Davie finally arrived and Pooh was thoroughly irritated. He was allergic to being on time. She sat in the passenger side of his car with her arms folded over her chest. “So where we going?” She was hopeful that he had a plan.

“To the movies,” he said.

She dropped her arms and looked over at him. “Davie, I can’t be going to no movies. Them kids is out here somewhere, and I’m gonna have to find them right now. Not later. You said you would help me.”

“Look, for once in your life let me be the man,” he smiled and her heart melted.

Davie was stunningly attractive despite his erratic drug addiction, and stupidity. He kept his hair cut low and his gear fresh at all times. Truthfully the only thing missing on Davie was his brain.

“Now I got a plan that’s gonna work, Pooh. We gonna go to the movies, check out that flick both of us wanted to see and when we get back the kids are gonna be in the room. Trust me, I know this.”

“How they gonna get in though? I didn’t give them no key.” She looked at the frost on the window. “It’s cold as shit out here, and they don’t even have no coats on. What if somebody snatched them?”

“Now who’s talking high?” He grinned.

Pooh was still waiting on an answer.

“Listen, Pooh, the peoples at the motel gonna let them in,” Davie continued. “They kids and they gonna open the door so they can be safe until you come back. I’ve seen this type of thing a million times,” he beat his chest. “Trust, Davie for once in your whole life! I got this.”

Pooh had no idea how she let Davie convince her into going to the movies. Not only was he talking through it the entire time, getting on everybody’s nerves including hers, but considering the children were missing, it was bad taste, and a waist of time. Not to mention she kept farting and sending egg scents throughout the theater, because she was so nervous.

When her cell phone vibrated in her pocket, she shitted in her drawers before even seeing who it was. She didn't bother to get out of the theater to handle her business. Nothing was more important than seeing who was hitting her up at the moment. She just knew it was Kimi.

With the phone in her hand, she saw it was her mother asking her to bring her a pack of cigarettes over from 7-Eleven, along with a bag of salt and vinegar potato chips. Kimi reached her wits end, and could no longer stand idly by. She stood up and said, "We gotta go, Davie. And, we gotta go now."

"Sit the fuck down, bitch!" Someone yelled in the back of the theater. "Can't nobody see shit over that big ass head!"

"Nigga, who is you talking to like that?" Davie asked, ready to box. He leapt up and stared in the direction of the voice. "I ain't say nothing about that silver back ape with a purse you brought up in here!"

"Hold up, what you just say about me?" The woman said standing.

Before Davie could respond, the woman had thrust all four hundred pounds of her body weight onto him, sending Davie's back crashing to the steps. Pooh called herself hitting the ape on her back but she didn't seem fazed. When Pooh assumed things couldn't get any worse, the ape's boyfriend walked up to the back of Pooh and came crashing down on the back of her head with something hard.

The last thing Pooh remembered was dropping, she was out cold.

Pooh was in the hospital looking at a white male doctor with a serious glare. “Miss, what happened to you tonight?” His voice was kind but serious. “You are in pretty bad shape.”

She popped up straight in the hospital bed, and looked around the room. A hospital was the last place she wanted to be at the moment. “Where is my boyfriend? Davie?”

The doctor immediately seemed annoyed, and she knew Davie had gotten to him already. “He’s in the lobby, unfortunately we had to make him wait out there after he kept demanding that we give you a pregnancy test.”

Pooh frowned. “What? I’m not pregnant.”

“Well he seemed to think you are. He kept saying something about him not wanting to be a father.”

She was embarrassed, and rubbed her sore head. “I don’t understand why he would do that, but I’m sorry.”

“Truthfully we don’t know what got into him either. We told him you passed out due to a blow to your head by the handle of a weapon. He thought it was something else.”

Pooh’s head was thumping, and she finally remembered her problem. Cordon and Miranda were still out in the world, all alone. While she was at the hospital, she wasn’t even close to finding the kids and solving the case. “I gotta go,” she moved to get off of the bed when he placed his pale hand on her arm.

“Ma’am, we can’t let you do that. You suffered a head injury and…”

Pooh pushed the doctor so hard, he went flying into his chair, and rolling back into the wall. She caught wheels as she ran out of the doctor's office, and into the lobby trying to get free.

Davie was reading a magazine until he saw her in a hurry. "What's wrong? You pregnant?" He shook his head. "I told them doctors that was why you passed out, but they threw me out thinking I didn't know what I was talking about. I knew I was right though."

"Davie, you gotta take me back to the motel. I can't play these games with you anymore. I gotta find out if they back or not and I gotta find out now."

"I'm on it!"

When Pooh and Davie walked into the motel room, and Pooh saw their coats right where they left them, her knees weakened. She fell to the floor and cried long and hard because they had not returned.

The harder she sobbed the more the stiches in the back of her scalp itched. In order to stop the bleeding, the doctor shaved a patch the size of a golf ball in her scalp and sewed her up. It wasn't pretty at all. But with her adrenaline pumping, she didn't even know it was that bad until she got into Davie's car.

"Somebody took them," Pooh sobbed. "They took Cordon and Miranda, and I'm going to die. The worst thing you can do in the world is lose somebody's kid."

Davie dropped to his knees and did his best to soothe his erratic girlfriend. "No they didn't. They black kids, baby," he said stroking her back. "They not in right now. If folks is stealing any kids out there, it would be them white ones. Trust me."

As dumb as Davie sounded, she really hoped what he was saying was true. But she couldn't get over how cute both of them were. Cordon, with his smooth chocolate skin and drug dealer son physique. And, then there was Miranda. Her vanilla skin and her long black hair, which ran down her back, in Pooh's opinion, made both of them marketable.

"What if you wrong?" She asked sincerely. She just knew some creep would see them and be in pedophile heaven. "What if they were kidnapped?"

He sighed, "Then we gonna have to find a way to get you out of the country. Sooner than later."

That was the realest shit he said all day.

"Do you kids need a ride?" a pretty black woman asked, pulling alongside Cordon and Miranda as they walked down the street. "You shouldn't be out here alone. This highway is extremely dangerous."

Miranda looked at Cordon. When they first started their journey he'd asked her to let him lead, and she was trying to but she was just like her mother in some ways. Strong. Bull headed and often stubborn. Still she remained silent.

"No, we don't need a ride," Cordon told her with a polite smile. "Our parents are in that car up there," he pointed up the street at no vehicle in particular. His chattering teeth, due to the cold weather, hindered his speech.

The woman seemed frustrated at his response. "Are you sure, young man? Because if I hear about something happening to you later, I'm not going to be able to live with myself. My schedule is clear for the day and I don't have any problem taking you both home."

He smiled kindly again. "It's okay, ma'am. We're fine."

When she pulled off Miranda pouted, and folded her arms against her chest. "Why didn't you let us take that ride?" She looked at her car as if she would turn around. "That's the fourth one we passed up. If we wait too late, we gonna die out here. Plus I'm really cold now."

Cordon tried to find the right words to say to her. If someone were listening to his heart they'd discover that he was beyond scared. He didn't want to be in charge of any of this and part of him resented Miranda for placing him in such an awkward position, when she suggested they'd leave the motel earlier. But, he was growing up, and figured if he could get both of them to safety, and back to their parents, she would like him even more.

"We didn't take the ride because I didn't trust her," he walked up the street and she followed him. "We gotta wait on a better ride."

"But she was a lady," she sighed. "And she was real nice. Nicer than the other men who tried to pick us up."

Cordon stopped next to a blue Ford pickup and faced her. "What did you see strange about the other men, when they pulled up on us?" He rubbed his itchy red nose and waited on her answer.

"What you talking about?" she rubbed her arms trying to get warm.

"I'm asking a simple question, when the other men pulled up, what did you see?"

She shrugged, and looked up at the darkening sky. Just like when she was in school, she was desperate to give the right answer. "The first man, in the white-like car, had his son with him…I think. Both of them smiled so I didn't see a problem with him. They looked nice to me."

"Did you see the way the boy looked at us?" he rubbed his nose again because it was starting to run. "The way he smiled, didn't look funny to you?"

Miranda smacked her tongue. She hated when he talked like an old man. "I don't understand what you trying to say, Cordon."

"The boy looked scared, Miranda," he said seriously. "Like he didn't want to be with his father either. Like he was warning us to stay away. You didn't see that?"

"No," she said truthfully.

"Now what did you notice about the other two?" Cordon continued, desperate to prove his point.

"Well the second man in the red truck I didn't like at all. He seemed like he would hurt us or something."

"See…so we do agree on some stuff," Cordon smiled. "And what about the other man? Before the lady just now?"

Miranda wrecked her mind. "I don't know…um, he seemed nice too. He was white and everything."

Cordon wasn't sure what that meant but he said, "He looked at you the entire time. You didn't see that?"

"So," she shrugged, "people look at me all the time."

"Well he was looking at you while I was talking to him. My daddy always says to watch what people do with their eyes. I didn't like his and I didn't feel safe. So since I'm in charge, I didn't want us to go with him either."

Miranda thought he was doing too much considering they were alone and no closer to their parents. The weather was unmerciful and it was getting dark outside. He didn't want them asking strangers to use the phone. He didn't want them going to stores to speak to strangers. He didn't want them to do anything but walk and she had the impression he was scared of everything and everybody.

"So what about the lady?" Miranda asked him.

"She had a beer in her lap," he said nodding. "It's not cool to drink and drive and I didn't want you to get hurt."

"But we gotta trust somebody," she yelled at him. "We need to use the phone."

"And we will use the phone. When we meet the right person."

Irritated with his response, Miranda stomped ahead, and Cordon followed. "So what, you mad at me now?" He asked her.

"I don't know what I am," the air from the cars speeding by her made her even colder. Her face reddened at the low temperatures, and she coughed repeatedly. "I mean, I think I'm scared now."

Cordon's heart dropped. If she was scared, it meant she thought he couldn't protect her. And, if he couldn't protect her, maybe she wouldn't like him anymore. "We gonna be fine, Miranda. I promise."

She rolled her eyes, and felt guilty immediately. If he didn't want to be her friend anymore she would be sick, but as it stood, the evening was not turning out like she planned. They walked up and down the streets, and because Cordon's father told him not to trust strangers, he didn't like anybody he met.

"Cordon, maybe we should go back to the motel," Miranda said in a low voice. "I'm thinking my idea to leave was bad now."

His eyes widened and he stepped closer to her. "You told me that you get straight A's in school."

She smiled. "Never had anything lower than an A in my entire life."

"So if you so smart, then why you trying to go back on what you thought?" He paused and grabbed her hand. "You said you heard her say something creepy and so we had to leave. I don't think we should turn back now."

They continued to walk up the street and Miranda asked, "You ever been lost before?"

Cordon searched his seven-year-old mind. "I don't know about lost, but I felt like something happened to me when I was real like little. Something that don't make sense so I never told nobody before."

They walked past a lady and her dog. "What was happend?"

"I don't really know where I was," he shrugged. "And I can't remember a lot, but I think I was a baby or something. And I was taken from this lady."

"A lady?" she said softly. "She wasn't your mother?"

"I don't know," he answered honestly. "I can't really remember any faces. I just remember it being night, and me being really scared. Like somebody was taking me away from somebody I loved." He looked over at her hoping he didn't sound too weak. "I sound dumb right?"

"No," she shook her head rapidly, before letting a heavy cough exit her lungs. She wiped her mouth with the back of her hand. "I read a lot of..."

"I know...*really big books*," he said mocking the way she talked. She giggled and he nudged her softly with his shoulder. "I'm just playing. Go 'head though. What was you about to say?"

"I can be irritating sometimes huh?" Miranda asked holding her head down. "Kids get mad at me all the time in school."

"I don't think you irritating. I was just playing. I think you are the opposite," he held her had softly. "So tell me about what you read in them big books."

"Oh yeah, one time I was reading in an encyclopedia that some babies can remember things in their first week of life. Within hours of them being born," she seemed suddenly sad. "Maybe you remember something people wanted you to forget," she coughed harder. "Maybe it was about your parents."

"Are you okay?" He was beyond worried about her. "Your cough sounds like it hurts."

"I'm really cold, Cordon," she looked at him. "I need to warm up for a little bit."

Cordon looked to his left and saw a house. It was a beautiful cream-colored house with large trees. It was neat, and appeared warm although he never went for outside appearances. "Let's go over there to that house to see if we can use the phone."

She beamed. "Thank you!"

They walked toward the house and when they stood on the steps, someone opened the door before they had a chance to knock. Although Cordon was immediately paranoid when he saw the man's face, Miranda wasn't.

The creepy old man had extra fluffy grey eyebrows and matching nose hair. His eyes were really tiny, making it difficult for Cordon to read him. Even if he could see his eyes, his vibe immediately made him uncomfortable. But Miranda, whose cough was getting worse, looked at the older black man's warm smile and felt relief.

"Well hello there? Are you kids okay?" Mr. Creepy said looking at the children. "What can I do you for?"

When he opened his mouth, and Cordon saw his yellow teeth, Cordon immediately wanted to run. The old man felt off. Way off.

"Can we use your phone?" Miranda asked. "To call our parents?"

"Miranda, maybe we should go down the street a little further," Cordon said, pulling her hand, "our parents are probably back at the store now. Let's go wait on them."

"No," she snatched away from him. "We gotta use the phone now and I don't want to go anywhere else," she combatted. She could feel the warmth in his house from where she stood along with spotting his baby grand piano. It was the most beautiful instrument she'd ever seen in person.

"Wait, are your parents with you?" He looked behind them. "Or are you lost?"

Cordon remembered what Flex told him. Before giving a response to any inquiry, he needed to consider the question.

In Cordon's mind there were only a handful of reasons why Mr. Creepy would want to know where their parents were. And one of them was that he was probably up to no good.

But, before Cordon could respond Miranda said, "Yes, we're lost. So can you help us?"

Cordon felt gut punched.

The old man grinned and said, "Well come on in. Mi casa es su casa."

CHAPTER SIX

THE NEXT DAY

Kimi sat in the corner of Cash's house laughing her face off. Flex spent hours torturing her and still he'd come up with nothing. Kimi held onto the information she had about Cordon's whereabouts, tighter than a pair of vice grips.

Quita, in an attempt to save Kimi from Flex's bullet, tried to contact Pooh, knowing she'd do anything to help her cousin. She couldn't help but wonder if Pooh had Cordon. The plan ended in vain when Pooh failed to answer the phone.

So with no more information than when they started, Flex thought it was better to proceed with his plan of punishment, as opposed to no plan at all.

Quita was weakened by all of this. She loved Kimi dearly and couldn't understand her mindset at the moment. Part of her understood why she would be so angry and deny Flex of Cordon's location. Had Quita been lied to, in the same way Kimi had, and had her child removed from her at birth, who knew how she would have reacted. Still, she was seeing a side of Kimi she hadn't seen before. Was she a mother scorned? Or a monster? Was Cordon safe or was he killed like she'd done Cash? Quita couldn't say for sure.

"You need to know that I got a whole lot of shit planned for you," Flex threatened as he cracked his knuckles. "And if you don't tell me where my son is, and soon, it's gonna get worse before it gets better."

Flex hoped she was buying his bullshit. Because the truth was, although his database of torture schemes was thicker than the Yellow Pages, he didn't have the energy to carry them out. Kimi had taken all he had to offer, and had yet to part her lips about where Cordon was.

And with the sun shining through the windows now, it marked the first day that he'd ever spent from Cordon. He was emotionally and physically weakened by his son's absence. Kimi's plan to break him, whether she knew it or not, was successful. He was done and was no longer thinking straight.

"Give me all you got, Flex," Kimi laughed, bloodied, beaten but not weakened. "Can't you tell? I can take it. I can take it all."

"Why would you want to do this?" Flex asked in frustration. "If you really believe you have a right to be Cordon's mother, why would you want him out there without help? Don't you care what may be going on? Don't you care about where he might be? This is ridiculous!"

"Of course I do, Flex. I care about him more than you could ever know. He's my son," Kimi said with spit flying out of her mouth. "But I also would rather see him dead, than for you to be with him another minute. I told you that already."

He frowned. "And you wonder why I took him from you," he tried to jab at her core like she was jabbing at his. Something about her expression told him it wasn't working. "This is why I separated him from you. Dumb shit like this. I knew when I caught you selling pussy in that strip club that you weren't fit to be a mother. And I was right."

Quita was stunned. From the moment she met Kimi, Kimi always played herself off as someone who was well rounded. Now Quita was finding out her darker side.

"You didn't give me a chance to be a good mother," she laughed, although she was hurting. "You don't know what I was capable of. You used my womb as an incubator because that barren wife of yours couldn't even give birth to weeds," she laughed wildly. "Not even if somebody stuffed them between her legs."

"Kimi," Quita screamed knowing this may be what sent him over the edge. "Don't do this shit!"

It was too late. Flex leaped up and choked her so hard, she passed out.

When Kimi came to, she was laying in the bed. Quita and Flex stood at the foot of the mattress.

"Kimi, I don't want to hurt you anymore. I really don't," Flex seemed more humble even though she wasn't buying it. "I'm willing to co-parent our child but I can't do that if I can't find him."

"Why did you wake me up?" she asked in a husky voice. "I wanted to die." Kimi rubbed her head. "I was in heaven and everything. You should've seen it. It was me, and Cash," she grinned and stared at the walls, "and he wasn't mad at me anymore for killing him." She focused on Quita, knowing she would be familiar with the story. "I'd forgiven him for raping me and everything," she smiled again. "It was so beautiful, Quita." She focused on Flex. "The funny thing is, I asked about your wife when I was in heaven, and she wasn't there. I'm not sure, but I think she's in hell, with the rest of the weaklings who take their own lives."

That was it, Flex grabbed her by the back of the hair and pulled her out of bed. "I'm sick of your shit, bitch! If you want to play rough, I'll play rough. I see now I can't talk any sense into you!"

"Flex, please don't do this," Quita pleaded following him toward the front door. Kimi's body was knocking over everything in its path as he pulled her as if she were a cavewoman and he was her man. "If you kill her we'll never find out where Cordon is."

Flex was unmoved. His goon, Morton, opened the door as Flex pulled Kimi to the curb. She was limp and wasn't defending herself. She'd given up and that scared both Quita and Flex. Because if she'd given up, it meant that he may never find his son.

Flex placed her mouth on the curb, and slammed his foot down into the back of her head. The sound of her teeth cracking could be heard. Blood and teeth splattered on the curb and Kimi passed out cold, again.

Quita covered her mouth in awe looking down at her bloodied friend. She was certain that Kimi was dead this time. "Oh my God, Flex," she looked down at Kimi's bloodied head again. "What did you just do?" Quita looked at him. "We'll never find Cordon now. You just killed her! Why?"

"Take her into the house, Morton," he said ignoring Quita's questions.

Morton quickly lifted her body and hoisted her into the house, away from prying eyes. Flex removed a handkerchief from his pocket and wiped the blood off of the bottom of his jeans. He had so much blood on him that the stains remained.

He looked out into the neighborhood; to spot witnesses and no one seemed to be looking in their direction.

"I've done that a thousand times," he winked at her. "You can think of me as somewhat of a pro."

"But you stepped on her head," she said shivering. "Hard."

"She'll be fine, although she'll have one hell of a headache when she wakes up from this one."

Quita's phone rang off of the hook in her pocket. By this time in the morning, she would be accepting her first child at her daycare center. But, at the moment, she didn't care who was calling her and for what. She was not leaving her friend alone with that maniac. She knew staying around could be hazardous for her own health, but when her mother died, as far as she was concerned, she died too. Quita assumed she had nothing to live for.

When one of the callers left a message, she decided to remove it from her pocket and listen.

'Quita, this is Cruella. I called like I always do, to see if you're up before I drop off my baby, but you not answering. I hope everything is okay. Pick up the phone. Zaboy has a new routine he wants to do for you and the children at the daycare center today. He's very excited about it. I swear this child is a star,' she giggled. "*The routine is with Survivor by Destiny's Child. He's so adorable. Anyway, call me back.'*

Yuck! Just the thought of Zaboy doing anything for her made her stomach rumble. Five-year-old Zaboy, who was extremely irritating, did stupid shit like ask for food others wanted, just to throw it away and say it wasn't good.

To make matters worse, Kimi nicknamed him Mr. Show Tunes, because he sang songs he learned from the

Glee Club at his school. He wasn't talented and forced people to listen, even if they didn't want to hear the noisy ballads. He also kept a fresh case of strep throat or pink eye on him at all times, which gave people more reasons to avoid him.

"You need to go open up the daycare center," Flex said walking up behind her, as she sat on the edge of the bed looking at her friend. He overheard the voicemail. "Ain't shit you can do for Kimi now."

"I'm fine," she stuffed the phone back in her pocket. "I never closed the center since it's been in operation. I'm allowed to miss one day if I want to. And, nothing is more important than this right now."

"I need you to open that center," Flex said seriously. "You no good to me here."

Quita stood up and looked at him. "Go to the center for what? My mother died, my friend is hanging onto life and Cordon is God knows where. If I go home right now, I won't be able to concentrate anyway. I'm better off here."

"I don't need you worrying about Cordon. I'm doing that enough for everybody. What I need you to do is leave and open that center. My boy knows your information. He knows your address, and he knows your phone number. I just got this phone the other day and I don't know if he remembered it or not." Water formed in his eyes but his expression had not changed. "I'm not asking you, I'm telling you to go home. If he calls your house, I want somebody to be there to take it it."

She looked at her friend once more. Kimi's lips were the size of two hot dogs and her teeth were jagged. If she survived, she'd need thousands of dollars worth of dental and plastic surgery, just to look normal again.

"You know, before all of this, she was a really good person," Quita wiped the tears that crept up on her face. "And I have to tell you, even though she didn't say it, I don't think she did anything to harm Cordon. To tell you the truth, I don't see how anybody would do anything to harm him. He really is a loving kid."

"She did do something to him."

"What was that?"

"She took him from his father," he wiped his hand over his face and walked to the other side of the room. "The moment I took Cordon into my arms, I made a promise that I never broke until now. And, that was to never go to sleep without seeing his face. That's why I'm cautious with the things I do and the people I let him meet. He's never not been with me so I'm sure he's losing his mind right now not knowing what's going on. I didn't even tell him I loved him, before I dropped him off at your daycare center."

Despite the extreme tension, Quita thought of a light moment. "Cordon knows that you love him. I can see it in his eyes when he talks about you."

Flex grinned at the thought.

"But, how do you think he'll feel when he learns that you killed his mother?"

He glared and rushed toward her. "His mother committed suicide."

She backed up. "His mother is lying on that bed, Flex. You and I both know it," she sighed. "If nothing else, let us not forget Charlene. And, her wishes."

"What the fuck is you talking about?"

"Your wife wanted Cordon to be with me so he could get to know his biological mother. So he could get to know Kimi. Denying him of that opportunity is like stealing from your own child, Flex. You're mad right now, but when you get him back, it's important that you remember that."

"She never told me that she wanted Kimi to have a relationship with Cordon."

"Maybe because she knew you'd act like this," Quita responded. "He will hate you forever, if he ever found out about what you did to his biological mother. I promise you."

"That's one person's opinion," he stepped back and looked at Kimi. "Right now, I need you to do what I asked. Go and open the center. And to tell you the truth, I'm not in the mood to ask you again."

She grabbed her purse and walked into the doorway. "Why do you trust me? What's to stop me from telling the police?"

He laughed at her. "The only thing I know for sure is that you not crazy enough to call the authorities. You can't risk being the blame of Kimi or Valencia dying. And there's one other thing," he said looking into her eyes, "for some reason, I can tell you really care about Cordon. When I came here last night, I had plans to kill you immediately, but that fact, was the only thing that saved your life."

She swallowed realizing now how close she'd come to death. "Can you promise me something, Flex?"

Silence.

Since he didn't respond she continued. "Can you promise me that you won't kill her before telling me?"

"Even if I did, you wouldn't be able to talk me out of any decision I make," he told her.

"I know, and I'm not trying to do that. I just wanted an opportunity to say goodbye. That's all. I've been knowing her all of my life, Flex. This isn't somebody who I just met the other day. We were very close and I can't help but think that had she told me about what she was going through, that I could've been there for her and none of this would've happened."

"Then maybe it should be you lying in the bed instead of her."

She swallowed. "I'm not saying it like that."

"It doesn't matter because I'm not in the promise making business anyway, Quita. If I couldn't keep a promise to my son, what makes you think I give a fuck about you?"

CHAPTER SEVEN

Maine was irritated with Valencia. She called him out in the living room three times, and each time he walked out she didn't want shit. He wasn't her fucking waiter, yet he was feeling like it. If Valencia didn't want something this time, he had all intentions of slapping her back to a newborn baby.

"What do you want, bitch? I'm not fucking around with you no more," he stood over top of her as she sat on the floor.

Valencia tried to appear sexy by opening her legs, poking out her breasts, and fluttering her eyes. But, she looked like she was trying to get something off of her eyeballs instead of seducing a man.

"I think my arms are tied too tightly," she winked. "You mind helping me out a bit?"

Tech sighed. Her terrible skills were making him weary.

Truth be told, Leroy was unimpressed also. Their freedom depended upon this moment and Valencia acted like she was a rookie.

"I told you what I would do if I came out and you misled me again didn't I?" Maine stepped up to her and she could smell the sweet scent of weed on his skin.

"I'm not misleading you. My wrists really are too tight," she said as if he gave a fuck.

"You're either fucking with me or you wanna get hit."

She was about to part her lips to pick her answer but he placed his rough finger over both of her lips and pressed hard. "Before you answer, let me tell you where both of them lead you. If you're fucking with me," he removed his gun from his waist and pointed it at her head, "I'm going to shoot you." he pressed the gun against her lips and stuffed the barrel into her mouth. "Now if you want to be hit, I can help you out with that too." He cocked the weapon. "Which one is it?"

"I want to be hit," she said, trying to smile.

He removed the gun from her lips, stood up and smiled down at her. Then he slapped her so hard, she was staring at the front door. Five minutes later, when she turned her head back, he was gone.

Valencia looked at Leroy and he shook his head. "If you can't seduce that fat mothafucka, you must not be worth shit in the bedroom."

Valencia tried to rid herself of the ringing in her ears that remained from Maine's crucial smack down.

"That nigga was all on me in my house yesterday, and now he's acting different." Valencia ran her tongue over her dry lips. "Maybe he don't wanna bite because of ya'll."

"Me?" Leroy chuckled, exposing his missing teeth. "I'm not the one trying to get him interested in my pussy. It seems to me that you need a few pointers on what a man likes."

She sighed and tried to sit up straight. "It's nothing you can tell me about giving away pussy that I don't already know. If he ain't interested now, he won't be interested ever."

"You all wrong," Leroy laughed. "Did you see the nigga's eyes? He's tweaking. The two things he wants in this world are food and pussy right now. You just have to tell him what he needs because it's obvious he's too fucked up to know for himself."

She sighed and rolled her eyes. "So I'm supposed to just come out and tell him I wanna fuck? That ain't seducing and that ain't what I'm 'bout. You got me all the way fucked up."

"You not taking him out on a date. You're trying to get him in the room," Leroy looked her straight in the eyes. "Now do you want my help or not?"

What Valencia wanted was for him to shut the fuck up. Better than that, she wanted Flex to step to him about what he did to his wife. She figured he wouldn't be so smart mouthed if he knew what his own son had in store for him. But instead of telling him how she really felt, she asked, "What do you got?"

"Tell him you have to go to the bathroom, he'll have to take you and best of all, help you take your clothes off," he looked at her pussy print again. "If your theory is right, with the two of you alone, there's no reason he won't go for it."

She crossed her legs and said, "What's sexy about that?"

"It ain't about it being sexy. It's about opportunity," he sounded like a real perv and she hated him more. "Have you taken a look at your boyfriend lately?"

Leroy nodded in Tech's direction. His eyes were closed.

"He's not going to be able to make it much longer like that," he losing too much blood. "This is our only hope."

Valencia gazed at Tech and her heart ached. If he weren't wheezing, she would not have known he was alive. "I don't know about this."

"Then you must want him to die. Because if he doesn't get to a hospital and soon, he'll be an afterthought."

Valencia thought about her life. She had been warned about this moment and it was coming to pass. Some month's back, Valencia met with Bula, who was a psychic. Bula predicted her brutal future, but she also told her to stay away from Tech. This was right before Tech convinced her to kidnap Leroy, in an attempt to extort money from Flex.

Because Valencia didn't heed her warning, she was tied up, smacked silly and looking across from a suspected rapist. Her life at the moment was the pits.

With nothing left to do she said, "I'll do it."

"That's good," he said unenthused, "but from where I'm sitting you don't have a choice or much time. I suggest you move on it now."

Valencia took a deep breath and thought about how to call Maine again. She knew she needed to say she had to go to the bathroom and ask for his help. But he'd given her two options already, and she didn't hear a third.

Suddenly she felt like she wouldn't be lying by saying she had to use the bathroom because she had bubble guts. So she put her big girl panties on and called is name again.

"Maine," at first her voice was a whisper and Leroy took the liberty to let her know she wasn't loud enough.

"He's not going to be able to hear you like that," he said cutting his evil eyes at her. "You gotta call him louder."

Oh how she hated that man. She took another look at Tech who was breathing slower. He was her motivation. "Maine," she screamed scaring Leroy.

Maine waddled into the living room with a new attitude. He was determined at that moment to choke her out. "I got a feeling I'm 'bout to kill you."

Valencia swallowed and tried to smile. "I'm sorry, but this time it's serious. I'm not trying to irritate you."

"So what, you're admitting that the last few times you were fucking wit' me?" he asked stepping closer until he was standing over her again.

She looked up at him. "No, it's just that, I have to use the bathroom. Really bad."

He laughed. "You sitting down already, get to pissing."

"But I'm on the floor," she said as if he wasn't aware. "And I'll mess up my jeans."

He raised his eyebrows and asked, "And you want me to give a fuck why?"

"Because I gotta shit too," she blurted out. "And although a pissy smell might not extend to the back where you are, a shit smell would." She tried to look innocent. "Please let me go to the bathroom, Maine. I'll be quick."

Maine considered her for a moment, and snatched her up by the elbow. Since her ankles and wrist were tied, she hopped like she was in a potato sack. Mad at her and the world for making him miss a re-run of "Martin", Maine pulled the door open and threw her to the toilet. With wide eyes she sat down and looked up at him.

"I can't pull my jeans down myself," She looked at them. "I need help your help, Maine. Can you pull them down for me?"

Maine sighed. "Fuck…I'm sick of this bitch," he said as if she wasn't there. He picked her up like a rag doll, snatched her pants and then her panties. Then he threw her down on the toilet seat. "Now shit!"

Valencia was so scared she was trembling. Her legs jiggled and she looked down at her bare feet.

"Are you gonna shit or not?" Maine said growing angrier.

"I can't concentrate with you standing right there," she said as she gazed up at him. "Can you give me a few minutes alone?"

"You either shit, or don't," he shrugged. "But I'm not leaving out of this bathroom unless you coming with me."

"Why do you hate me so much?" she said trying another approach. "When we were at my house I thought you liked me. You even offered me a pull from my own weed after you rolled a blunt. Remember? I thought we was friends."

"We were never friends," he told her strongly. "I tried to be, but you weren't trying to fuck wit' a nigga. You remember that shit?" he leaned against the door. "I knew you wouldn't give a nigga a chance though. Bitches like you only want a nigga when they don't have another option."

"That's not true," she tried to convince him. "You and Tech were in my house and I was scared I was about to die. I didn't know what was going to happen. You try being in my situation and then tell me how you would handle it," she sighed. "Look, Maine, I know you don't like me, but we're going to have to spend some time together, the least we can do is be friendly with one another."

"What if I don't want no new friends?"

"I'd want you to at least give me a chance. Please," she pulled his belt loop. "I been looking at that fat dick all day. How about me and you play a little, before we part ways."

Silence.

Maine didn't say anything. He just looked down at her like she was a roach waiting to be squashed.

She knew then that the dumbest move she made yesterday was giving him a hard time. But hindsight was twenty-twenty and it wouldn't help her at the current moment. She needed him to bite now. She needed him to be interested. And if it worked, maybe she could free herself and Tech too. She could give a fuck less about Leroy's toothless ass.

"I ain't fucking wit' you," he told her straight up. "I don't like bitches like you because I don't't' trust you. Now either shit or get off the toilet." He reached down and yanked her hair, "And just so we're clear, I'm not telling you this anymore."

Maine pushed her head back and released her hair.

Valencia lost it. She finally lost her sex appeal. She couldn't even get ugly ass Maine to want some of her juicy. To make shit worse, she had to sit on the toilet and produce a bowel movement that wasn't there.

"Hurry the fuck up, Valencia," he nodded waking her out of her thoughts. "I got places I'd rather be."

A warm stream of piss exited Valencia's pussy and slapped into the water. She was happy something came out because at least she wasn't lying about having to go. When she was done pissing, she bared down as hard as she could but nothing else would come out. But what did enter into her head was a new plan.

Valencia adjusted a little on the toilet and looked up at him again.

"What you looking at?" he asked. "You looking real sneaky."

"Nothing," she smiled.

"Well hurry the fuck up before I slap the shit out of you again."

She put her head down, looked at her feet and wiggled her toes. On ten she would make a move and go for what she knew.

One. Two. Three. Four. Five. Six. Seven. She looked at his crotch area. *Eight. Nine.* On ten, she charged after him head first, and bit down on his dick. Whether he knew it or not, she was determined to get out of that bathroom and eventually out of the front door. Even if she had to have a piece of his dick in her mouth.

Quita sat on the edge of the bed looking at a picture of her mother in her bedroom. The sunlight sneaking in from the window shined on her mother's face, and she tilted the photo to see her clearly. She looked so beautiful and peaceful.

She thought about her demise, at the hands of Flex. At least dementia didn't haunt her anymore and she wondered if death was the best thing for her. A tear fell from her eye and dropped on the framed picture. She wiped it off and sat the photo down.

Looking out of the window, she thought about her life. What a fuck up she'd become. She couldn't see things getting any worse until Zaboy came into her room singing, proving her wrong.

'Starlight, star bright, first star I've seen tonight.' It was Madonna's old song *Lucky Star*.

When Quita didn't appear to be listening, Zaboy came around to her side of the bed and did a little dance. His suspenders had his brown corduroys, hiked so high, that his baby nuts looked like a big clit.

'You must be my Lucky Star', he continued to sing. *'Cause you shine on me wherever you are.'*

Annoyed, Quita slammed her chunky hand over his lips and pressed, "Shut the fuck up! I don't feel like hearing this right now!"

His eyes spread wide and he frowned.

"Now when I remove my finger you won't be singing anymore okay?" When he didn't nod she said, "Zaboy, do you understand me?"

He nodded and she took her hand down. He gave her a dirty look and he said, "My mother said my ears are for God's purposes only. You not supposed to be cursing around me. She done told you that already."

"I'm a grown woman, Zaboy," she stood up and walked toward the bedroom door. "I do what the fuck I want. And I told *you that already*."

"I'm really telling now," he promised hanging by her side like a third leg.

She rotated her head from left to right. The last thing she was thinking about was Cruella's mustache having ass. If she wanted to get on her for cursing in front of Zaboy, she could take her son and leave. Because both of them knew not a daycare center within the state would have Zaboy.

"Where is Clarkita?" she closed her bedroom door and he followed behind her, stepping on the back of her ankles in the process. "And stop walking so fucking close to me! Damn!"

"She downstairs making breakfast," Zaboy said excitedly. He hopped around like the floor was hot. "She told me to come get you because it was time to eat."

Quita descended the stairs and walked toward the kitchen. "What is she making?"

"Some pancakes and bacon. I told her I wanted five," he wiggled the fingers on his right hand, "and she made them for me. You can't take them back either. They mine."

"You are so fucking annoying," She told him secretly wishing she could slap the shit out of him. Zaboy was too grown.

"What did you say?"

"Nothing, Zaboy."

When she hit the corner, the sweet smell of maple bacon was overpowering. Normally she would be elated, but today her stomach was doing somersaults.

Clarkita was in the kitchen pouring warm butter over the pancakes and placing them on the table. Her beautiful baby Axel, was giggling loudly at his dog that was licking his feet.

Baby Axel use to be a major headache for Quita at one point in their relationship. Because as cute as he was, he didn't like humans. He cried when you didn't pick him up and he cried when you picked him up. He cried so much that one day a fly flew into his mouth and almost choked him to death. He was a little ball of nightmare.

It wouldn't be so bad if he didn't lure you to him with his deep brown camel colored skin, curly hair and shiny brown eyes. But bet money that the moment you had him in your arms, he would wail so loudly you'd be likely to throw him on the ground.

That all changed when one day, Quita was taking all of the kids out for a walk in the park. She was with her assistants Pooh and Essence. Things were cool until a yellow pitbull, off the leash, charged in their direction.

Not thinking straight, and on instinct, Quita took off running with the kids while both of the assistants followed. The only problem was, she left the baby in the stroller. Sadly the only one who tried to save Axel from the pitbull was Cordon. He had enough bravery to at least grab a branch, in an attempt to defend him. But when the dog finally got up on Axel, instead of chewing his face off, he licked his forehead, and the baby threw his legs up in glee. Quita had never seen Baby Axel that happy before.

With Axel's hands and legs on the dog's nose, he was in heaven. No more crying and no more tears. Quita used the opportunity as a growing moment and went out and bought a yellow Lab the next day. She told Clarkita how to quiet her baby, since prior to that moment, nobody wanted to watch the kid. When it was all said and done, Quita essentially saved Clarkita's social life too.

"How are you feeling?" Clarkita said, pulling a chair out for Quita. "Sit down, and I'll fix you a plate."

"I'm not hungry," Quita said sadly. "I don't feel too well."

"But I'm hungry!" Zaboy yelled crawling into the seat at the kitchen table. "And I want five pancakes."

"You not gonna eat five pancakes, Zaboy. Start out with one."

Hearing the bad news, he cried at the top of his lungs. Both the baby and dog participated in the crying song sending Quita's temples into full thump mode.

"OKAY!" she screamed. "You can have it." she looked at Clarkita. "You can give him whatever he wants."

Clarkita Kemp, 42-years-old, despite her grey Jerri Curl, was beautiful, single and alone. She had Axel after being inseminated in a fertility clinic and he was her only child. Unlike some of her other clients, she was a board certified surgeon who pretty much wrote her own ticket. She was kind, willing to give her all and that went for everybody she met. Quita couldn't count the number of times Clarkita would stay late to help them clean up the center, since her baby was often the last to go home.

Clarkita fixed Zaboy's plate, kissed her baby and rubbed the dog's head.

Quita smiled. "Did you name the dog yet?"

"We call him Hero," she shrugged taking a seat next to Quita. "Because he saved the day. I got a date lined up tomorrow and now my friends don't mind watching him too on the evenings you can't."

Quita smiled. "That's hot." She looked over at the dog and baby. "At least somebody's happy," she sighed. She looked at the clock on the wall, "Why aren't you at work?"

"Because your mother died and you need me." She sat next to her and placed her hand over Quita's. "And I would want somebody to be there for me if I needed them."

"But don't they need you at the hospital?" Quita asked although she really didn't want her to go.

"The hospital has lots of surgeons," She looked around Valencia's house. "But judging by the look of things, you don't have too many friends around here. I think my time would be better spent here."

Quita cried heavily and placed her face on the table. "Thank you so much for staying, Clarkita. I don't know what I would do without you right now."

Quita discovered recently that Clarkita knew her mother before she got sick. They went to grade school together and remained pretty good friends for years. Quita discovered that they talked about her all the time and how smart she was. Quita's heart warmed hearing the information the other day, especially considering her mother was no longer around mentally.

Before her mother was killed, Quita saw her once a week, no matter what. She would've loved to have told her mother that Clarkita entered her life but she never got a chance. Thanks to Flex.

"You won't have to worry about doing it without me because I'm here," she paused. "So what's going on with your friends? Kimi and Valencia?"

"Kimi is bad." Quita wiped the tears off of her face. "Flex is beating her unconsciously because she won't tell him where Cordon is. And Valencia is still held up at Tech's house. I don't know the status of her."

"Why he beating her like that?" Zaboy said entering the conversation without a pass. "That's not nice."

"You're not supposed to be in adult conversations," Quita yelled at him. "Now eat your food before I make you go upstairs."

Zaboy frowned, took a bite of one of the pancakes and said, "Yuck! I don't like these pancakes. They nasty!" he hopped down from the table, grabbed his plate and threw the plate and food in trash.

Quita ran up to him preparing to knock him into the stove until Clarkita grabbed her hand. "Zaboy, why don't you go on downstairs with Essence. I think I heard her say she's about to play the *Toy Story* movie for you."

Zaboy moved for the basement but stopped short and said, "I'm going to tell my mother on you! You been mean to me all day." he pointed at Quita. "Watch!"

She was about to charge him again but he dipped down the stairs just in time. "I don't know about this shit." Quita told Clarkita. "I don't think I can watch kids no more."

Clarkita turned blue. She needed Quita's help with baby Axel. Not only because no other daycare would watch him, but also because Quita loved him and takes the best care of him. "What did I tell you the other day?"

Quita shrugged. "I got so many things going on right now, that I can't even remember my name some times."

"I told you that I know that you love money and there's nothing wrong with that. But there ain't nothing you can say, that will convince me that a person who chooses to deal with the worst kids money can find, would do this for so long, accept for the fact that they are an angel from God."

"Clarkita, please don't."

"It's true. This is your calling, Quita. You handle the misfits and the children forgotten. And whether you know it or not, you were put here to help parents like me. Don't give up on me now. Please."

Before Quita could respond, there was a knock at the door. She was afraid that it was Flex telling her that he just killed her best friend. Instead, when she turned the knob, she was staring at Miranda's beautiful mother, Vonzella.

Her light skin was red due to the cold air and her long hair flew everywhere. The blue jeans she wore hugged her curves and her ass was so perfectly round it looked fake. The bruises on her neck were still visible and Quita guessed that it was from her crazy boyfriend Mike, abusing her.

Mike stood by her side and his red Lexus was parked on the curb. His energy was dark and it made Quita uncomfortable. He was wearing the same black North Face coat she saw him in when they first met.

"Girl, please forgive me," Vonzella said. "I'm sorry I'm just picking Miranda up right now." She looked at Mike. "Me and my baby were out all night and when we got up, it was the next morning. I'll pay you for the time though."

Quita looked at Clarkita to see if she was as confused as she was. And Clarkita looked equally muddled.

"What are you talking about?" Quita asked. "Miranda ain't here."

The fake smile on her face cracked. "What do you mean Miranda ain't here?" she looked at Mike and then back at Quita. "Your assistant Pooh came and picked her up, saying she was getting her for you."

Quita couldn't believe her ears. She was right. She had a feeling Pooh's greedy ass may have been involved, but when she didn't answer her mother's phone, she chalked it up as a lost cause.

"Yeah, we figured she wanted to spend some time with that rich ass kid so we let her go with the chick," Mike added. "Matter of fact, where he at?" He was always concerned with Cordon and he gave Quita the crawlies.

"He's not here and neither is Miranda," she looked at both of them. "I think you must be mistaken."

Mike stepped up to her so that his coat was touching her breasts. "I really hope you're not playing games with me." His hot breath kissed her nose.

"I'm serious. Miranda is not here," Quita responded.

"Well, I think what you got is a mothafuckin' problem!"

CHAPTER NINE

Miranda sat at the piano and played Moonlight Sonata by Beethoven. Although Cordon had no idea what the song was about, since he preferred rap, the creepy old man was delighted.

"Oh my dear, Miranda," he said, his thick grey eyebrows moving with a life of their own. "You played that beautifully," he cheered, holding a tray full of sliced brown bananas in his hand. "Where did you learn to play?"

She closed the piano's lid and said, "I taught myself."

"Please don't stop." He begged. "Play some more."

She produced a half smile and coughed. "My fingers hurt," she wiggled them, "and I don't feel too well."

"Just one more piece," He persisted sitting the tray down. "Please."

"She said her fingers hurt," Cordon said from the table. Miranda had been playing the piano all night and all morning and he knew she was tired.

The Creepy Man frowned at Cordon and his jaw buckled. It wouldn't be unfair to say that he wasn't a Cordon fan. "Very well," his grin was fake, "if the young lady is tired, the young lady is tired." He looked at her. "Why don't you come on over here and eat."

Miranda strolled toward the table and sat next to Cordon. Both of them looked up at Mr. Creepy.

"Can we use your phone now?" Miranda asked. "It's the next morning and our parents are going to be worried sick about us."

"But you have to eat first," he said pointing at the food. "I sliced these for you."

Cordon looked down at the brown bananas and his stomach churned when he saw one of his gray eyebrow hairs sitting on top of it. "I'm really not hungry," he said.

"Me either." Miranda admitted.

Mr. Creepy frowned and said, "Either you both eat, or you can't use my phone." The niceness had gone. "Now I'm trying to be good to you, but I have to tell you, I don't like how either of you are treating me. Did you learn any manners from your parents or from wolves?" he said loudly.

"From my mother," Miranda said weakly.

Mr. Creepy laughed. "It's no wonder why both of your parents didn't come looking for you. You're both shiftless kids."

"I have manners," Cordon said under his breath. "And she does too, but I don't think you're being fair."

"Being fair?" he said stepping closer to him. "Did you just say I'm not being fair? When I let you into my home and tried to feed you," he nodded at the tray of ugly fruit. "Is that how you feel too, Miranda?"

"Yes," she said softly.

Mr. Creepy bit down on his bottom lip until it bled. As they watched blood drip from his mouth, they wondered what he was about to do to them.

"You know what, it doesn't matter what you think is fair," he sucked the blood off of his lip. "This is my house." He looked at both of them. "And I let you both into my home." He was breathing so heavily that his nose hairs flew in and out of his nostrils. "So please enlighten me on how I'm being unfair." When they didn't respond he roared. "TELL ME!"

Miranda shivered but Cordon sat firm. He was also frightened but he remembered what his father said, to never let them see you sweat. "You're unfair because you said we could use your phone, but you didn't let us use it. All we want to do is call our parents and go home."

Mr. Creepy looked at them angrily and then smiled. "Is that all?" he laughed slapping his hands together. "Because if that's it, I told you I'll let you use my phone, but only after you eat." He pushed the tray over to them. "And I mean every last slice." He walked into the back of the house and left them alone at the table.

Miranda started sobbing and Cordon's heart rocked. He pulled her to him and rubbed her arms like he saw Flex do his mother when she was upset. "Please don't cry, Miranda. We gonna be fine."

"But he won't let us go home," she continued.

"Maybe he will," he rubbed her harder. "We just gotta do what he says."

"But what if he doesn't?" she pulled away from him. "What if he doesn't let us use his phone? And let us go home?"

He didn't have an answer. "We getting out of here," he smiled at her although he didn't believe himself. "Just don't cry anymore."

Miranda slid the tray toward herself and frowned. Then she grabbed one of the banana wedges and shivered, as she was about to stuff it into her mouth.

Cordon snatched it from her and ate it himself. He could tell she didn't want them. "I don't want you to eat this stuff," he whispered. "I'll do it."

One by one Cordon stuffed the sludgy mess into his mouth, even the one with the hair on it. When he was done, he called out into the grim house, "We're done!"

Mr. Creepy came back outside and looked at the tray, not a single slice was left. "Well, it looks like somebody was hungry," he said slapping his hands together.

Irritated Cordon said, "Can we use the phone now?"

"Yes you can."

They both smiled.

"But first I have a surprise for you both," Mr. Creepy announced.

"We don't want a surprise," Cordon told him. "We want to use the phone."

"Are you her boyfriend or something?" he questioned gritting his teeth. "If you not, you sure act like it."

"She's my friend."

"I figured as much," he shook his head. "Boys like you when I was growing up always got the girl, but they never knew what to do to keep them. I use to take boys like you out back of the school, and make them pay for teasing me."

"I just want to use your phone," Cordon continued.

"And I said you will after you answer me honestly," he smiled again. "Do you like surprises or not?"

"I don't like them," Miranda replied.

"How come I don't believe you?" Mr. Creepy walked to her side of the table. "I bet a pretty little girl like you gets all sorts of surprises." He picked up the locket she wore around her neck, opened it, and looked at the picture of a piano. When he flipped it over he saw, *'From Cordon to Miranda'.* He looked at him. "Seems to me like you two are more than just friends."

"We just kids," Cordon reminded him. "And we just friends."

He laughed. "Well since you're kids it means that I'm the oldest. And since I'm the oldest it means that I'm in charge. And I'm telling you that I have a surprise for you both that you will love. After my surprise you can go home," he slapped his hands together again. "So, give me a second and I'll get it together."

"Can you at least tell us what it is?"

"Let's just say if you like the movie the Lion King, you're going to love the surprise." He disappeared into the back of the house leaving them alone.

When Cordon couldn't see him anymore he turned to Miranda. "We have to get out of here now. If we don't he's going to hurt us."

Miranda was shivering. "But I'm scared. What if he comes back and catches us."

"We can't worry about that right now," he looked down the hallway. "We really gotta go." He pulled her hand and moved toward the door but she pulled him back. "I'm scared."

"Miranda, then come with me," He pulled her again but she snatched him back. "What's wrong?"

She was shaking so hard he couldn't understand what she was saying anymore. "I d…don't, wanna…wanna…."

He yanked her harder and moved toward the door anyway. The doorknob twisted and the cold air smacked them in the face. They were about to walk out when Mr. Creepy came behind them and slammed it shut.

"Where are you two going?" he seemed confused at both of the kids. "I was planning a surprise for you and this is how you repay me?"

"We just wanna go home," Miranda cried. "Please let us leave."

"Unfortunately I can't do that, my sweet, Miranda," he said, softly. "How about we go to the back now. I want to show you both my surprise."

Cordon and Miranda reluctantly followed Mr. Creepy to the back room. Miranda was sobbing softly and it must've irritated Mr. Creepy because he slapped her so hard she fell down.

Angry, Cordon hit him in the arm but he pushed him off.

"You know what, I'm getting sick of you two," Mr. Creepy yelled. "I'm trying to be nice but I'm not going to play this game much longer. Now if you both don't straighten up, I'll show you the bad man I can be," he continued breathing over their heads. He looked at Miranda. "Now get up!"

Cordon stood up and he helped Miranda to her feet.

Mr. Creepy wore a smile again. He removed some keys from his pocket and opened the door. The moment it opened, the smell of sweet incense smacked them in the face. From Cordon's view, he could see a large bed with a gray comforter on top of it. There was also a video camera on a tripod.

"Go inside," Mr. Creepy instructed.

Cordon didn't move and neither did Miranda.

"I'm not going to tell you two again."

They trudged into the room.

"Go sit on the bed," Mr. Creepy commanded.

They obeyed.

"Are you gonna ever let us call home?" Cordon asked again.

"You want the truth or another lie?"

Cordon's heart dropped and Miranda started weeping louder.

"I thought we were going to watch the Lion King," Cordon replied.

"I got a better idea," Mr. Creepy slapped his hands together again. "Instead of watching a movie, I'm going to make both of you stars."

Maine's sweat dripped on the back of Valencia's head as his body pressed against the bathroom door. Every time he moved slightly, she would bite down harder on the jeans stuffed with his dick.

"Valencia," he said softly now trained on what would happen if he moved too quickly, "please stop doing this. You can't begin to understand the pain I'm in right now."

"I tried to give you some pussy," she said although her voice was slightly muffled, "but you didn't want it." From the closer view, he could see he didn't have his gun on him. This couldn't be more perfect.

"I want it now," he cried softly. "Please give it to me now."

Valencia tried her best not to laugh. Even if she was interested in taking him up on his fuck offer, he wouldn't be functional for at least a week. "Sorry, nigga. The pussy is off the table now," she said contemplating biting harder. "What about that shit you were kicking earlier? About slapping me? What do you think about doing that now?"

"Valencia," he said softly with his hands out to his side so that she wouldn't think he was about to harm her, "I'm sorry about hitting you earlier. I really am. But you gotta understand, Flex put me in charge and I didn't know what you were trying to do when you kept calling my name."

She squeezed his dick harder and he screamed out. "So you lying on Flex now? Huh? You trying to tell me that Flex told you to hit me? I could tell by the look in your eyes you loved that shit!"

"No he didn't tell me to hit you, but if you tried to escape, that would be my head if you got away." He was sweating so badly now, it was as if a water faucet was turned on. "I liked you from the beginning, Valencia. I told Flex and everything but he told me to keep my head in the business. So when you stepped to me, I couldn't move on it." He was about to weep.

"What else he tell you?" she paused and repositioned herself on her knees, "and if you lie to me, I'm gonna bite this mothafucka off, Maine. Tell me everything you know."

"I don't want to tell you," he said softly, "because you might take it out on me."

"I want you to tell me the truth." When his hands dropped a little she yelled, "hands up, nigga! I'm not fuckin' around with you!"

His hands flew up like a flag on a pole. "Okay, okay, I'll tell you everything. Flex said to hang by the phone for his call, and he said that when he gave me the word, that I was to finish the three of you off."

"You mean to kill us?"

"Yes," he said trembling. "But I didn't want to do it, Valencia. I liked you."

As Valencia sat on her knees, with a mouthful of jean covered dick, she considered her predictment. Essentially Maine confirmed what she'd always known. When it was all said and done, Flex wouldn't be releasing any of them, including his own father.

As much as she hated to admit it, she was happy that Leroy and Tech pressured her into seducing Maine. Sure it didn't work out the way she wanted it. And sure he turned her down. But, at the end of the day she was getting the result she wanted even though the plan had slightly changed.

"When is he planning to kill us?"

"Once he finds his son," he responded. "On my mother's heart, everything I said just now is true." He was in so much pain, he was experiencing body chills. "Valencia, I told you everything you wanted to know. Are you going to let me go now?"

She shrugged and the movement caused her to clinch his sack harder again. "I don't know."

"I won't do what he's asking me. I promise," he cleared his throat. "Now can you please let my dick go. I'm about to pass out."

"This is what we're going to do," she said as her voice vibrated into his balls, causing him more pain. "You're going to untie my arms and ankles, and you're going to do it real slowly."

"Okay, the moment you let me go, I'm going to untie you," he responded eager to put this all behind him.

"Aw, no you don't nigga," she replied. "You're going to bend down, and you're going to untie me first. I'm going to keep your dick as collateral until my arms and legs are free. When they are, I'm going to let you go. Deal?"

"But if I bend down, I'm going to be in more pain if you don't let me go."

"Then you must want us to stay like this all night," she said in a deep tone. "That's on you. But I gurantee you I can do this longer than you can take it."

"Oh my, God!" he screamed out realizing that no matter which way he moved, he was still in a fucked up situation. "Why are you doing this to me?"

"What the fuck you want to do, nigga? I'm not about charity and I'm not about playing with you. And since you were so inclined to give me two options outside, one of which resulted in me being slapped, I'm going to return the favor."

"Valencia, please. I'm about to pass out."

"Hopefully you'll hear your two options before you do." she paused. "Option one, you take this rope off of my arms and let me free. Or option number two, I chew this mothafucka so hard, you won't be able to do shit with it but look at it. Am I clear?"

"Yes," he sobbed like a little girl.

"Good, now what option you want?"

"Option number one. I-I'll take option one."

"I think that would be best," she said sarcastically. "Now you gonna move slowly and I might tighten up a little, just so your dick won't leave my mouth, but I'm not going to bite the mothafucka off. You have my word."

"How do I know you not?" Maine asked in a shaken voice.

"You gonna have to trust me," she said maintaining control of the conversation. "Now bend over and release the ropes.

Maine slowly bent down and began to unravel the ropes around her arms. Just as she promised, the tighter grip she put on him had him feeling lightheaded. But he pushed through it, hoping that soon it would all be over. When he finished, with the ropes on her legs, he dropped them and stood up.

Valencia breathed a sigh of relief. It was as if a five hundred pound man just stepped off of her chest. She rubbed her wrists but maintained her bite hold.

"I let you go," he put his hands up again as he looked down at her. "Can you please get off of me now?"

"I'ma do it," she said loving the power and fear in his voice. "Just give me a second to think about how I'm going to get out of here."

"Valencia, I'm not going to touch you. I promise," he begged softly. "Please let me go."

Valencia thought about her situation. As it stood, she was on her knees with a stranger's dick in her mouth. There were several things that could happen if she let him go. One of the things he could do was knock her out and go for the gun that she was sure was in the bedroom. Or she could bite him as hard as she could, watch him drop and get out of the house. Valencia wanted the last scenario so badly, she could taste it.

"Are you gonna let me go now?" he asked waking her out of her thoughts.

"Yeah, I'm about to get up now. You looked out for me so I'm gonna look out for you," with that she bit down on him so hard, she felt something pop in her mouth.

"Ahhhhhhhhh," he yelled as he fell toward the floor.

Valencia quickly moved out of his way, before he crushed her. His head hit the porcelain toilet bowl and he rolled on his back. Both of his hands were stuffed in between his legs, as he cried wildly.

Pulling up her jeans, she rushed out of the bathroom and headed toward Tech's bedroom on the hunt for the gun. She could hear Maine bumbling around in the bathroom and knew time was not on her side.

When she pushed Tech's bedroom door open, she saw a rack of adult magazines spread out over the bed. She lifted them up and looked under the pillows but still she saw no gun.

"Where the fuck did you put it you, fat bastard?" she said to herself dropping to her knees.

She looked under the bed and in the closet but she didn't see the gun anywhere. Something told her to look in the pillowcase and when she followed her hunch, she was correct. She grabbed the silver .45 and charged toward the living room. Once there, she placed the gun down and untied Tech's arms and legs. She was beside herself when she noticed his eyes weren't opened.

"Oh my, God!" she wept checking his pulse. "Tech, please don't die on me." She couldn't feel a heartbeat. "I need you to be with me right now. Please." Once he was untied, she placed her finger on his neck. She couldn't feel a pulse there either.

"Look, the nigga is dead," Leroy said unsympathetically looking toward the bathroom. "Now come untie me so we can get out of here."

"Nigga, fuck you!" she cried. "I'm not leaving here without him," she continued to check his pulse like it would miraculously come back.

"I know you have feelings for that nigga, but you gotta worry about the living right now. Because if we don't get out of here, we gonna be laying down there with him," he looked toward the bathroom again. "You need to come on over here before that nigga come back from whatever you did to him and want blood," when Valencia hadn't budged he said, "what are you waiting on?"

She frowned at him. "Why should I help you out?" Spit hung out of the sides of her mouth. "You ain't nothing but a selfish ass man."

"You can run, but you can't hide," he said through his missing teeth. "You should let me go because when my son gets back, he's going to come looking for you. And whatever problem he has with me, will be resolved. He's about family, Valencia. But if you let me go I'm going to vouch for him to leave you alone. I know my son. He'll listen to me. He always does."

Valencia looked down at Tech and saw he was a lost cause. Crying the entire way, she crawled to the other side of the living room, toward Leroy. "Turn around," she told him.

Leroy spun around like a top and Valencia removed his ropes. His flesh was rubbed so raw on his wrists, it looked like he was wearing pink bracelets. Once he was free, she rushed toward the door. She tripped over the couch but got her bearings together. Her heart beat in her chest and it seemed like the door was too far away to touch.

When she finally made it to the door, she realized she didn't have the key to get out. To make matters worse, she felt her life stop when she heard Leroy's words.

"I'm sorry, sexy, but I'm not going to be able to let you leave out of that door. I really hope you can understand," he cocked the weapon she left at Tech's side, in her haste to leave. "So how bout you turn on around, before I put a hot ball in the back of that pretty little head of yours."

She turned around slowly and looked at him in disgust. She couldn't help but cry as she leaned up against the door. She trusted a rapist and now she was paying with her freedom.

"Are you serious? I let you go, Leroy," she threw her hands up in the air. "Why are you doing this shit to me?"

"This ain't about you, beautiful," he looked her up and down. "Although I sure love to look at you."

"Then what is it about?"

"You don't need to know all of that," he walked toward her, gripped a fistful of her hair and threw her onto the sofa. Tech's body rested at her feet. "You just need to worry about me, and what I might do to you if you make any strange moves." He looked down the hall again. "I gotta know though, what the fuck did you do to him to get him to untie you?"

Silence.

"I understand why you're mad at me," he walked into the kitchen and picked up the phone on the wall.

Valencia tried to think of a plan to attack him and leave again. But her plan was split. He had the gun and Maine had the key to the front door in his pocket.

"If I were you, I'd be mad at me too," Leroy continued.

"This is so stupid," she told him. "And you're going to pay for it too. I'm sure of it."

"Maybe, maybe not." With the gun aimed at her he dialed the number. There was a long pause before he said, "Son, it's your father." he paused again. "We had a situation over here. Don't you worry about it though, I have it under control," he winked at Valencia.

CHAPTER ELEVEN

"You know I use to love you so much," Kimi told Flex although her jaw was swollen and inflamed. Unfortunately Flex didn't do as much damage as he would've wanted. "Even when I look at you now, I remember the good times. It's amazing the kind of control you have over me."

He sighed and sat at the foot of the bed. He didn't bother to tie her up, because her legs were broken and he was certain she couldn't move even if she tried. He broke them in his latest attempt to get her to talk. It didn't work.

"Kimi, why are you doing this? I just don't understand it. I mean, do you wanna die?"

"You can't understand what it means to live your whole life with guilt. The guilt of not being there for your son and the guilt of not protecting him. If you did, you'd know that nothing you could do to me physically, could get me to change my mind."

"But he's a child, Kimi!" he said with a raised voice. "A kid. You know what kind of things go on in this world," he pointed at the window. "Do you want him to experience that side?"

"Why would you take my only son? Why would you do that to me? Didn't you ever stop to think how I may have felt?"

The pain she felt from her jaw and broken bones was so excruciating, that it caused her to sweat profusely. She wiped the wetness off of her forehead before it entered her eyes.

"I never lived a full life because I always wondered how life would have been with my son," Kimi told him. "I imagined how his eyes looked. I imagine how his arms would feel around me. You cheated me out of the motherhood I deserved and I'm angry about it. Guess what though, I have a right to be."

"I didn't mean to hurt you, Kimi. And I know it's hard for you to understand that, considering your current condition, but it's true."

"Then why do it?"

"Because Charlene couldn't have kids. And I loved her more than I loved anything or anybody. And even with her being gone, I still love her now," he shook his head and looked down at the floor. "We even tried from the beginning of our relationship to conceive, when we both were in high school. But it never worked."

"Then maybe it wasn't meant for you to have children with her. All things considered, she did kill herself."

"You don't understand," Flex said. "She came from a southern background and I came from a big family. We wanted the same for ourselves. So later in our marriage, we tried again but it didn't work. As much as we use to have sex, for some reason, we were never able to make it happen."

"So when you met me, you knew all along what you were going to do?"

"Yes."

Through squinted eyes she said, "You really are a monster aren't you? You have to be."

"You call me a monster but did you get a chance to look at your son?" he asked staring into her eyes.

"Did you see how healthy he is? How bright he is? I did that Kimi! I am a good father! Cordon doesn't want for anything, and I made a home for him."

"But you made it without me!" she cried. "And the fact that you can't see the good, leads me to believe that it doesn't matter to you."

"It's not that it doesn't matter," he said softly, "it's just that it doesn't matter anymore."

She frowned. "And what does matter?"

"Bringing him home. Reuniting him with me and the rest of his family. He has cousins, grandparents and everything else, Kimi. A lot of people will be devastated if he doesn't come back home. They love him. I love him."

"He has a grandmother on my side too!" Kimi combatted. "And she was cheated out of having that bond. Your family isn't the only thing that matters, Flex. Don't forget that."

"Kimi, you talking about shit that's irrelevant! Don't you see that nothing we talk about will change the past?" he stabbed his fist into his palm. "The only thing that matters at this point is making sure he has a full life."

"Let me ask you something," she readjusted herself in the bed. "Did you ever love me?"

"Why would you ask me something like that right now?"

"Because I need to know."

"I never loved another woman, outside of my wife. I told you that," he held his head down and looked into her eyes. "But I cared about you."

"And what the fuck is that supposed to mean?" she yelled.

"It means that had I not cared about you, and thought that there was some part of you decent, I would not have been able to fuck with you. Although I knew you wouldn't be in his life, I didn't want a mother for my son who was mean, or cold, or crazy. I chose smart."

"I can't believe this is happening to me," she closed her eyes and then reopened them to look at the ceiling. "I'm not a bad person. I have good in my heart. I just don't understand why I will never be able to be a mother to my son."

"Who says you can't?"

She looked at him. "I'm not dumb, Flex. I know you will never, ever let me raise him. As a matter of fact, you won't ever let me see him. The only place I'm going when I leave here is in a coffin," she smiled.

"See, you don't know me," He told her. "Think about it, my wife wanted you to be in your son's life. Why wouldn't I want her to have that? Even in death?"

"What are you talking about?"

"Before she killed herself, she wrote a letter. In it she said that it was important that Cordon go to Quita's daycare. I never understood why because she didn't tell me anything. I didn't even know she knew you and Quita ran a center together. Anyway, I know she did that so that he could know his biological mother."

Kimi wasn't impressed. "I guess years of lying and manipulating must've worn on her."

"You have to be careful with me, Kimi," Flex said softly. "I'm a man who has lost his wife and can't find his son. I can't have you talking to me so recklessly.

Now if we are going to work this out, we need to talk, minus the shots at my wife."

She rolled her eyes. "Say I believe you, about wanting me to be in Cordon's life, what's the plan for Cordon? He's going to take this hard."

He sighed. "Well, I think we need to ease him into the fact that you're his mother. Moving too quickly may scare him and confuse him even more. When he's older, maybe in middle school, then we can tell him the full truth."

"Even how you stole him from me, in the back of some stores?"

"I can't do that. I still want a relationship with him too you know."

Kimi seemed hopeful since he rattled off a plan. "But how do you think he'll take me being his mother? I'm sure he loved Charlene a lot."

Flex sighed again. "He's going to be hurt," he stood up and leaned against the wall. "He'll probably be mad at me for lying to him too. But I'm sure we can work through it, especially after I tell him why we did it."

"I'm not sure the reason for you stealing him from me, is strong enough to justify what you've done, Flex."

"I know, but it's my only plan," he looked into her eyes. "Tell me where he is, Kimi. Tell me where I can find him."

Kimi closed her eyes and considered what he was saying. At one point she trusted him, and believed he didn't want a child. She learned years later that she was wrong. He was a good liar. She reopened her eyes. And now that she looked at him, again, she could recognize him for the man that he was.

"I can't do that, Flex. I'm sorry."

He was about to try another approach until his phone rang. He removed it from his pocket when he saw an unknown number. Believing that it could be news about his son, he answered. "Hello."

"Son, it's your father." Leroy said to him.

Flex was so angry that Leroy was able to call him that his skin boiled. As far as he knew, Maine had him, Tech and Valencia tied up and waiting on his call. So what happened to his order?

"What do you want?"

"We had a situation over here. Don't you worry about it though, I have it under control," Leroy continued.

Just hearing Leroy's voice put Flex in a different mood. In fact after he finished with Kimi, his plan was to be reunited with Cordon, make sure he was settled and murder Leroy. He still remembered when he learned why his wife committed suicide. It was during a conversation he had with Quita some time back.

"I need to know everything," Flex said to Quita, after learning that she may be privy to why Charlene killed herself. "About my wife."

"Well, she was raped by your father. He got her pregnant and she contracted HIV."

So the last thing Flex wanted, at the moment, was to be hearing Leroy's voice. "Son, are you there?"

Flex frowned. "Yeah...I'm here."

"What do you want me to do?" he paused. "Because I don't want you to have to worry about rushing back over here. You can handle your business freely, knowing that I got my eyes on Tech and Valencia and they aren't going anywhere. Plus I know that's what Charlene would've wanted since they may have had something to do with Cordon's disappearance."

Flex's breaths were heavy and he saw fire. Hearing her name come out of Leroy's mouth made it sound so dirty.

"Thank you for handling the situation," he said trying to keep a straight face and sound convincing. "Just don't let them leave, and I'll take care of you when I get there."

"Okay," he paused. "And son, I know you're probably mad at me, because of me using drugs again," he continued in a low voice. "I just wanted you to know, that this entire situation has awaken me. And if you can ever forgive me, I'm going to get some help and lead a straight life. That is why you're mad at me right?"

Flex wasn't aware that his father was doing drugs again. But none of it would matter in the long run because he still had plans to murder him.

"You found me out, pops. I was fucked up with you about that, but we gonna move past it," he looked at Kimi. "I gotta run right now, I'll holla at you later."

"Sure! Take care of your business."

"Great, and when I see you, I'll give you exactly what you deserve."

"Thanks, son."

Vonzella and Mike were now standing in Quita's living room demanding answers. They came to pick up Miranda and she was not there.

Quita could tell by the way Vonzella's boyfriend Mike had his hand over his waist, that he was about to do something violent. So it was time to come up with a lie and save herself.

"Vonzella, please forgive me," Quita said softly. "I've had a long night and I'm confused about everything. Of course I knew about Pooh having Miranda."

"That's right," Clarkita interrupted, "her mother just died and she just received some very bad news about her friends. Since then things have been moving fast and she hasn't had time to breathe."

"What the fuck does that got to do with us?" Mike said unsympathetic about Quita's plight. "My bitch came here to get her kid and she ain't here. Sounds to me like we got a problem."

"My situation doesn't have anything to do with you directly. But people make mistakes and I just made one," Quita responded hoping they both would believe her bullshit.

"Yeah, just like you guys were late coming to pick Miranda up, Quita made a mistake too," Essence said stepping behind Quita and Clarkita. "No worries though we can clear all of this up in no time." Essence's thick black rimmed glassed made her look studious and most of all believable. "I was just about to head over to Pooh's now to pick up Miranda and

Cordon. When I talked to Pooh earlier, she said they were eating breakfast."

Vonzella had been called out on her shit by Essence. Even though Miranda was not there, she could not help but think had they came last night, when they were obviously supposed to, her daughter would be there.

"How do I know you telling the truth?" Vonzella asked Essence.

"Because you gotta believe me," Essence replied pushing her glasses closer to her face. "I'm not a liar."

"Yes you are!" Zaboy announced coming from behind Essences' legs. You didn't talk to nobody today. You were downstairs watching the movie with me."

Clarkita was a nice woman. The kind of woman with principals and morals. But even she couldn't help herself when she slapped Zaboy on the back of the head, sending him flying to the couch.

"I'm tired of you digging into grown folks conversations," Clarkita said pointing her finger in his face. "As a matter of fact I been told you about that mouth of yours earlier today. Open your jaws again and I'm gonna make you feel more pain than you have in your entire life. Now take your ass upstairs," she pointed to the steps, "and wait in Quita's room." When he didn't move fast enough she said, "Do it quicker!"

For the first time ever, Zaboy didn't have a comeback. He was so scared, he fell two times before making it to the steps. Once he was there, he sulked all the way up the stairs until he was completely out of view.

Quita tried to hide her smile. Because although she watched the kids, she could never justify to one of the parents why she hit one. In her sleep she had visions of how it would feel to smack Zaboy. But Clarkita lived it. She was officially her hero.

"What was that about?" Mike asked Clarkita. "Why you have to hit the kid? He sounded like he was saying something we wanted to hear."

"And why would you listen to a kid?" Quita asked regaining control of the conversation. "Now we run this daycare center, and we're telling you that Pooh took both your daughter and Cordon to get some breakfast. If you came any later, you would've found us on our way to get them."

"Exactly," Clarkita added, "did you want us to call once we picked them up? It should take us about an hour."

"No, we staying right here," Vonzella said stuffing her fists into her hips. "And if ya'll don't come back with Miranda, I'm going to have to hurt something or somebody."

Quita's van was packed with Essence, Clarkita, Baby Axel, Hero the Dog and everybody's favorite villain, Zaboy. Quita had no idea if Pooh actually had the children in her possession but she was praying it was so. Besides, finding Pooh with both Miranda and Cordon would satisfy two parents at once.

"How you holding up over there?" Clarkita asked looking over at her from the passenger seat. "You look like you're about to explode any minute now. We can't have you doing that if you are. We need you strong."

Quita sighed. "I just can't believe all of this shit his happening right now," she raised a hand and dropped it back on the steering wheel. "Why is this happening to me?"

"We can't ask why once the damage is done," Clarkita sighed. It appeared like she went elsewhere in her mind. "This is the cross that you must bear. So bear it."

Just when things couldn't get any worse, Hero farted forcing everyone to cover their mouths and noses. Baby Axel on the other hand laughed hysterically.

"That baby is dumb!" Zaboy said, never missing an opportunity to be a little extra. "Him farting ain't funny. He stinks!" he pinched his nose so hard it turned red. "I can't stand stinky dogs."

Quita adjusted her rearview mirror so she could look directly into Zaboy's face. "Zaboy, I'm going to need you to be quiet. I'm sick of you being over the top, every time something happens."

He removed his hand from his nose and his nostrils popped back in place, "What's over the top?"

Quita was never asked the question before and was stuck when she couldn't explain it right away. She was so use to saying the phrase, that it just became second nature.

"It's like this," Essence volunteered, "whenever somebody says something, you don't have to make a response. It's quite all right to say nothing at all. And some conversations are just for adults and you not no man yet."

Zaboy couldn't wait until he got older so people could stop telling him that. "But if somebody is talking, ain't they looking for somebody to listen?" Zaboy asked the panel.

In his effort to seek the truth, he dropped some jewels in their laps and everyone was even more stuck.

"You're right, Zaboy, but the key word is *listen*. Just because they may want somebody to listen, it doesn't mean that they want you to respond," Essence continued.

"So it's like when somebody talk to they selves," he continued. "They don't really want somebody to talk back?"

"Exactly," Quita nodded. "It's just like that."

"Well I hate talking to myself," he said under his voice. "But I do it all the time, because I don't have any friends."

Everyone felt like shit for coming down on the kid hearing his situation. But he was like a pet dog that you had to take care of, but didn't necessarily like. And since Zaboy was so annoying, Quita didn't think that would ever change.

"Well maybe if you didn't talk every time somebody said something, then you would have more friends," Essence added.

"No I won't," he shook his head back and forth before looking out of the window. "Everybody hates me in my school. Everybody hates me around my house. And everybody hates me at Quita's," he looked around the van, "Even ya'll."

Silence.

Clarkita couldn't lie, the kid had a point. Everyone hated him and if he didn't change soon, he would get the same reception later on in life.

"So, Quita, how are you holding up?" Clarkita asked reverting the conversation back to her.

"I just want to find these kids over Pooh's mother's house. I don't feel like dealing with Vonzella or Flex anymore."

"Yeah, you have to be careful about Mike, too," Essence said. "He's not the kind of man you want to play with."

"Why do you say that?" Quita inquired looking at her through the rearview mirror.

"He's a stick up kid," Essence put her on. "As a matter of fact, my cousins know this dude he just robbed the other day. Mike and some niggas he was with shot him in the leg. He lost a lot of blood. Mike almost killed him. Now they looking for him and everything."

"Why didn't you tell me?" Quita asked her.

"I don't know," she shrugged. "When we came back from the park, and I saw Mike with Vonzella awhile back, I didn't have time to tell you. You told me to take the kids inside the house so you could be alone with them. But I don't think you have anything to worry about with Mike now that I think of it. He's only interested in people with drug money."

"That's where you're wrong," Quita corrected her. "I have everything to worry about, especially if Miranda is not over this girl's house when we get there."

****

Pooh's mother lived in Southeast DC, in a run down house. From the door, they could smell dirty clothes, weed and food at the same time. Quita knocked and could hear someone stomping toward the door.

"Who the fuck…" Theresa stopped in midsentence when she saw it was Quita on the other side. Although Theresa was happy to see her, Quita and her crew were thoroughly surprised at what she was wearing.

Theresa opened the door in some gold slippers, a white leotard, and a gold and white robe with feathers around the collar. Her hair was gold also and her long red nails added to the fuckery.

"Oh my fucking God!" Theresa screamed stomping her foot. "How come you didn't tell me you was coming over! Bitch, I was just telling Pooh about you the other day! I said she was some kind of stupid for losing that good job!"

Theresa's voice made everyone irritated but especially Quita. "You mind if we come in for a minute? I have to talk to you about something."

Theresa looked at Clarkita, Baby Axel, Essence, Zaboy and the dog and said, "Normally I don't like a whole lot of peoples in my house, but since I fucks with you hard, you can bring your fat ass on in here with your friends."

Quita shook her head at how ridiculous Theresa was acting and walked inside. The house was stuffed with so much junk, that there was literally an aisle that you had to walk through, just to get to the kitchen.

Once in the kitchen, Theresa removed stacks of newspaper out of each seat and they all sat down. When Theresa was finished, she laid eyes on Baby Axel.

"Oh my God!" her red nails moved to pick him up. "Bitch, this is the cutest baby I've ever seent in my life!"

The moment she had him in her arms, Hero growled, Baby Axel screamed in her face and the entire mood turned hostile. Theresa quickly put the baby back in Clarkita's arms and backed away from the dog.

With her eyes on Hero the entire time she said, "Now normally I don't fuck with no dogs. I hope you not gonna make me wish I hadn't changed my mind by letting him up in here."

"He doesn't bite," Clarkita said softly. "He's just overprotective of Axel that's all."

"Humph," she said placing her hand on her hips and leaning onto the stove. "He seems more than over-protective." She smacked her tongue. "The way he acting making me think they fucking."

"Theresa!" Quita screamed. "Why would you say some nasty ass shit like that?"

Theresa looked at everyone and saw they were frowning. "Oh my goodness, please don't tell me you done brought a rack of sensitive ass people in my house. Because if they worried about me saying something out of the way, they might as well leave right now."

"Theresa, we not sensitive," Quita corrected her. "We're just here on a sensitive matter that's all."

"Okay, stop beating around the bush and shoot it to me straight."

"We need to find Pooh," Quita told her. "Is she here?"

"Girl, that bitch done made me mad again!" Theresa said opening the freezer to remove a bottle of cheap vodka. "Do you know that I got my phone bill the other day, and found out that this bitch ran it up fucking with them niggas in jail? She done accepted a phone call from everybody in prison with a federal number." She poured herself a drink and didn't offer them a drop. "I had to throw that hussy out on her ass the other day."

Quita shook her head. "Damn."

"What's wrong with you?"

"Pooh took some kids and now they people are looking for them," Quita advised her. "I need to get a hold of her like yesterday."

"Ain't no need in you worrying!" Theresa announced. "I may not fuck with that bitch, but I know what and who my daughter is with at all times. I just got GPS on that phone she using of mine. Her's done got turned off. I checked it yesterday and she was at her boyfriend Davie's house."

"Can you tell me where he lives?" Quita asked in a hopeful manner.

"I can do better than that. I can take you there!"

CHAPTER THIRTEEN

Davie threw some water over Pooh's face, as she lie on the dirty motel floor, because she'd fainted for the second time that day. Every time she realized that she lost Cordon, and Miranda she would work herself up to a frenzy.

When Pooh regained consciousness, she spit some of the water out of her mouth and sat up straight on the floor. "What's going on?"

"You keep passing out," Davie said rubbing her forehead. "You gotta calm down though. You not gonna find them kids like this." He helped her to the bed. "We gonna find them though. I promise."

"But how, Davie?" she looked up at him for answers. "You been telling me this for the past day and we still haven't found them yet."

"Maybe we should call the cops," Davie said never thinking he'd hear the day he'd say those words.

"No! Because then they'll blame me," Pooh responded breathing heavily. "Do you understand what can happen to me, if Kimi and Flex know I lost them?" she asked, with wide eyes. "Flex is going to kill me! And Kimi might hold the gun for him."

Davie sat next to her. "Let's think hard," he said rubbing her leg. "Where do you think they could possibly go?"

"They could go anywhere," She said, shaking her head at his dumb ass question. "I don't know. That's why I'm asking you."

"Okay, when they left, where did they say they were going?"

"To the soda machine," she pointed at the door. "In the hallway outside of the room."

"Okay, how come we didn't check there already?" he asked seriously looking into her eyes.

"You playing right?" she inquired with lowered eyebrows.

"No, we should always look in the last place they went. So if they went to the soda machines, they could possibly still be there."

"Davie, we past the soda machines on the way to the room. There is nowhere for them to hide by the machine."

"Well I'm checking again."

Pooh watched as Davie inspected the soda machine. He looked to the left of it and then the right. He even got on his hands and knees and looked under it. When his brain engine really started to roar, he opened the soda slot and looked inside of there. With everything he'd done, Miranda and Cordon still were not found.

"Well," she asked sarcastically, "are they inside the machine or what? Maybe they miraculously turn themselves into a Coke or Sprite."

"You talking a lot of shit," he said standing up straight brushing his hands together. "You might not like my methods, but at least I'm trying to find the kids. All you want to do is pass out and cry."

Davie was right. People cracked on him all the time. They said he was stupid. They said he was a boat head. They even said he couldn't find his own eyes if he was looking at them in the mirror. But what people failed to say about him was that he had heart, and that it belonged to Pooh.

Pooh loved him just as strong. So much so, that when she found out that he slid off and got himself some neighborhood pussy one afternoon, she took it upon herself to crash his car windows.

At the end of the day, Pooh couldn't give a fuck what they said about him. She loved him and she was not leaving him. And at the current moment she needed his help.

"I'm sorry, Davie," she walked up to him and hugged him tightly. The smell of his Burberry Touch cologne made her horny. "I'm just so scared. What can we do now?"

"Get some weed."

She stepped away from him and said, "What?"

"You know I always think better when I'm high."

She shook her head. "If it will help, let's go."

Davie was on cloud nine as he smoked his weed dipped with Embalming fluid. He sat back in the seat of his car and took puff after puff.

As Pooh watched him enjoying life, she wanted to hit him in the throat but she held herself back.

She crossed her arms over her chest and pouted. Then she sighed real loudly hoping he would ask her what was up. He did neither. "Well..." she said looking over at him.

"Well what?" he kept his eyes on his weed and occasionally the road.

"Can you tell me what the plan is now?"

He took another pull. "Well, we can go to the store to get some liquor. Or we can go to my mother's house. I think she making some greens or something tonight. And if I smile real wide, she might fry some chicken wings and make her rum cornbread."

Pooh shook her head. He was dumber than ever since he just finished smoking. "I'm talking about the plan for finding Miranda and Cordon! Are you going to help me or not?"

"Wait, who is Miranda and Cordon?" Davie asked her, as he stopped at a light.

In a rage, Pooh pushed the door open, jumped out and stomped up the street. She was fifteen blocks from the motel and broke but she didn't care.

Davie caught her twenty steps out and pushed her against someone's brand new black Range Rover. "What are you doing?"

"I'm leaving!" she yelled in his face. "You not helping me at all right now and I'm sick of it!"

"Please don't do this shit to me!" he stepped back and rubbed his head. "Just give me a second to think. You know how fucked up I be, Pooh. I got a lot of shit I'm dealing with but I'm always there for you. You know that."

She looked at him and could tell he was about to cry.

"My mother is dying from cancer. My father is getting ready to get out of jail tomorrow and when he do, me and my brothers gotta do everything we can to keep him from our mother. Because even though he keeps beating her ass, she loves that nigga! Even though he broke her jaw fifteen times, because he thought she was smiling at different niggas. I'm fucked up, baby!"

Pooh felt her self about to cry. Now she felt like a broken heel for coming down on him so hard. "I'm sorry, Davie. I really am. I'm just confused right now and I literally don't know what to do."

"Okay, how about we go to Quita's house."

Pooh was confused. "Why would we go there? The motel is miles from her house. It's not possible for Cordon and Miranda to walk all the way there."

"What if they got a ride?"

"I don't know about that, Davie. It sounds risky."

"You told me that Cordon remembered Quita's address when you passed out and got locked up. You remember, the day you took the kids to the movies?"

Pooh was surprised he remembered and embarrassed that it happened. "How the fuck did you remember that?"

"I remember some things, when I try hard," he stepped back up to her and rubbed her arms. "I say we go over there and see if the kids are there."

"Why not just call?" Pooh asked.

"Because if they not there we don't want to be hot," he said rubbing her arms. "Instead of telling them that we looking for Cordon and Miranda, we just act normal. Did you leave anything over her house? That you can ask her for? We gotta have a reason to be there."

Pooh scratched her head and the stitches in the back of her head ached. "Not that I can think of."

"Well think harder. We want a good excuse to show up without letting on that we're trying to find Cordon and Miranda."

Pooh wrecked her brain and had a throbbing headache. The pain she was feeling from the stiches didn't help much either. When she was done going through her database she smiled. "I got it!"

He grinned. "What is it baby?"

"That fat bitch never gave me my last check," she hugged him tightly. "I can be going over there to get it from her!"

"I knew my baby would come through. Let's go!"

Davie cruised down the street and for some reason he didn't look high. "Thank you for everything, baby." Pooh told him. "You being here for me, and holding me down. It's like you're saving my life."

He winked at her. "You know I try not to promise you something and not follow through," he paused his thought.

"I know," she nodded.

"Well, I'm thinking about getting clean. I'm talking about not fucking with drugs no more at all," he sighed just thinking about the road ahead of him. "I don't know if I can do it though, but I'm going to try," he said honestly. "My mother just stopped smoking crack a year ago, when she found out she had cancer. And my pops never really stopped drinking. Addiction is in my family."

"If you try it, how are you going to go about doing it?" she asked sincerely.

"I don't know. Maybe put myself in one of them clinics," he shrugged. "I been waiting on my family to call the show *Intervention*, but ain't nobody did it for me yet," he laughed. "I just know I gotta do what I gotta do."

"Why all of a sudden?" she asked touching his leg. "You been getting high since I've known you."

"Because I want to marry you," he looked over at her. "And take care of you."

Pooh's heart thumped hard within the walls of her chest. She didn't just love this nigga, she lived for him. "Are you serious?"

"Yeah. I'm dead serious," he said looking out at the road ahead of him. "I know niggas don't think I can clean myself up. They think I'm gonna get locked up or be dead like a few other people in my family. But I'm gonna prove them wrong." he shook his head just thinking about the future win. "I might have to go away for awhile if I check into the clinic. I won't be able to see you. You gonna be able to hold that pussy together for me?"

There was no other nigga for her. "You know that. I'll never give you up. Ever."

"That's good for the nigga who would be stupid enough to fuck with you and for yourself," he squeezed her hand, "you belong to me."

"You don't have to worry about it. I'm good on all those niggas. I got who I want."

They were still shooting shit when Davie looked too long into Pooh's eyes and crashed into a truck. Their necks snapped back and forward violently. When Pooh opened her eyes, she was looking into a puff of smoke. When she squinted, she could see the back of a white BMW. The fucked up part was, she knew exactly who the vehicle belonged too.

Xtisha crawled out of her truck with her son Lil Goose on her side. Lil Goose use to go to Quita's daycare center, but was put out due to almost stabbing a kid.

Pooh could tell by the look on Xtisha's face that she wasn't happy to see her, and that the situation wouldn't end well.

CHAPTER FOURTEEN

"You are the dumbest, ugliest and greasiest nigga I know," Valencia said to Leroy, sitting on the floor next to her dead boyfriend. "Do you have any idea of what you're doing? You just sealed your own death certificate."

Leroy waved the gun at her. Valencia was nervous considering his finger was on the trigger.

"You don't know what you're talking about. I'm not the one who is about to die," he chuckled, "you are."

Maine still lied on the floor holding his nuts. He wanted to snatch Valencia's facial features off he was so disturbed. When she looked at him he said, "You better hope I don't feel a little better. Because if I do, I'm gonna get up and hurt you slowly. I promise you that."

She laughed. "As far as I know, ain't no nigga ever made it back from a crushed nut without a little help. The only thing you gonna be getting is a clit if they gotta cut that mothafucka off. You need to relax."

He tried to move on her, but the brutal pain kept him in place. She'd done a good job. "I promise, no matter what happens today, I'm gonna hurt you."

"Don't worry about it, Maine. I have her." Leroy said waving the gun some more and licking his crusty lips. "And the moment my son give me the SAY SO, I'm gonna plant all kinds of holes into this bitch."

She laughed. "You really don't get it do you?"

"What the fuck don't I get?"

"That your son doesn't fuck with you anymore. If he wanted you in charge, he would've put you in charge when he left out of here. You are dirt to him right now, Leroy. Live with it."

"Why do you think you know so much about me?" he laughed although he was starting to get nervous. He knew the call he had with his son earlier didn't feel right. "You aren't related to me. And prior to you kidnapping me with your dead boyfriend over there, we've never met."

"Don't even worry about that bitch," Maine offered trying to maintain a relationship with the new man in power. "She just a whore whose talking recklessly."

"And you just a fat ass nigga, one stop from being a bitch," she smiled so wide her pink gums flashed him. "Ain't a bitch alive who gonna fuck with you now. I saw to that shit."

He was trembling. "On my mother's heart…"

"Yeah, yeah, yeah! On your mother's heart, guts and eyes, you gonna get me," she mocked. "You can't even get yourself up right now, Maine. I crunched down on them nuts with force. Trust me when I say, if somebody's gonna get me, it damn sure won't be you."

"Well how do you know it won't be me?" Leroy said stepping up to her.

She wasn't smiling anymore. "Get the fuck away from me, Leroy. You gotta wait on your son's call remember? You can't touch me."

"Who said I got to wait on him?" he laughed. "I'm his father. He's not mine."

"Look, all I want to do is sit over here and mind my business. If Flex want to do something to me once he gets here, then that's on him."

"You haven't answered the question, smart mouthed, bitch," he said louder. "How do you know I won't be the one who teaches you a lesson?"

He put his paws on her breasts and she spit in his face. "Get your diseased hands off of me."

He backed away. How did she know he had HIV? "What you talking about, girl?"

"Look, just leave me alone okay? I don't want to bother nobody."

Maine laughed. "I don't know, Leroy. But if I was you, I'd go get some of that pussy before Flex get back. When I was in the bathroom with her earlier, that thing smelled just right."

Leroy looked back at him and grinned. "For real?"

"On everything. It smelled as sweet as baked bread."

Leroy looked back at Valencia and licked his lips again. "I don't know, sexy. I might be trying to test-drive that thing around the block just once. What do you say to that?"

Valencia was crying now. "Please leave me alone, Leroy. I don't want to do nothing but sit here."

"It's too late for all that," Leroy snatched her up.

"Why don't you let me hold the gun?" Maine said with both of his hands between his legs. "While you in the back."

"Not for nothing, my man, but it looks like you got your hands full right now." He walked out of the living room with Valencia's arm clutched in his grasp.

Once they were in Tech's room, he pushed everything off of the bed and threw her on top of it. Leroy closed the door and once again tied her arms behind her back, and placed his gun on the dresser. There was no threat.

"I'm gonna make this right for you, baby girl," Leroy told her looking down at her sexy body. "So there ain't no need in fighting."

"Leroy, please don't do this shit."

He gave her a fake sad look. "Why you say it like that? You make me think that fucking old Leroy is the worst thing in the world. Surely there could be worst things. Like dying." Leroy said.

"I'm not saying that. I'm just saying that I got a boyfriend."

Leroy tugged at her jeans until they were off and her pink underwear was showing. He rubbed his finger over the seat of her panties, and sniffed his fingertip. "Damn, he was right, that shit smells just right. And it's warm too."

She shivered. "How about we come up with another plan to get out of here?"

"You not reading the right paper, young lady," he eased into the bed and grabbed her foot. "The only plan on the table right now is you giving me some of this juicy. Now you can give it easily or I can take it. Which one you wanna do?" He placed her big toe into his mouth and sucked.

Her skin crawled. "You mean like you did Charlene?"

He threw her foot down. "What you talking about?"

"Flex knows, Leroy," he shot up and walked to the dresser. "He knows that you raped his wife and got her pregnant. And when he gets a chance, he's going to do something about it."

"Lies! I used a condom when I fucked that bitch!" He blurted out.

"So it's true?" she said covering her mouth. "Oh my, God! How could you rape your own daughter-in-law?"

He grabbed the gun. "I'm warning, you! If you keep lying on me I'll kill you."

"You can point that gun at me all you want. But you know I'm telling the truth. Now if you want to kill me on the strength of your lie, then there ain't nothing I can do about that and I won't try. But only you and her know knew what happened that day. Whether you raped her or not and now Flex knows too."

"So…that's why…"

"That's why he's gonna kill you," she said softly. "Think about his tone when he talks to you. He's done."

"But he didn't even hear my side yet," he said to her as if she could convince Flex to change his mind. "Nobody asked me anything."

Valencia shrugged. "Maybe he already believes her. And since she's not here to defend herself, he's probably really going to take her side. After all, why else would she leave her son?"

Leroy shook his head. "I…I can't let him think these evil things about me. I have to tell him that who-ever told him that lie is a liar."

Valencia scooted closer to the edge of the bed alt-hough it was difficult because of her hands being tied behind her back. "Leroy, he is not going to believe you. Trust me."

He frowned at her. "I'm tired of you thinking you know my family better than I do," he pointed in her face, "You don't know shit about me."

She leaned back and decided to go a different route. She was young, sexy and smart. She had to start using the assets God gave her, or else they would go to waste. "Can I be honest with you?"

Silence.

Since he didn't respond she continued. "I like you. I was attracted to you from the moment I saw your face."

He chuckled. "So what you trying to do now, use my own skills on me?"

She looked at him like he was out of his mind. "You didn't see how I kept my eyes on you all last night and this morning?" she opened her legs and flexed her pussy so that it pumped softly in her panties. "I want you to have this so bad, but I don't want to do it here."

He put the gun back on the dresser and took her panties off. Her heart was beating loudly because the last thing she wanted was him to plunge inside of her. And if she had a choice, she definitely didn't want him diving into her without a condom. Luckily she and Tech just bought a pack of condoms yesterday and they were in his dresser.

"Damn your pussy is pretty," he parted her lips and the pink center glistened. His fingers were dry until he flipped her juice back and forth and her juices spilled on him. "I bet you hear that all the time don't you?"

Leroy was about to eat her out until she scooted back and said, "You know what makes me smile?" He shook his head no. "To be finger fucked."

He bit his bottom lip. "Oh yeah, you like that shit, huh?"

"I sure do," she cooed. "So how about you give me two of them fingers now? Real hard too."

Instead of two, he gave her three. The pain was uncomfortable but you wouldn't know it to see her move. She twisted and popped her waist until every last one of his fingers was covered with her juices.

"Damn you look so good," he gripped at his dick in his jeans.

Valencia had to stop him. "Keep doing it, baby. Keep finger fucking me. That shit feels so good."

"I want to give you some of this dick, too."

"We can get into all of that later," she moaned as she twisted and turned some more. "Damn that feels so good, Leroy." she looked down on him and observed how he kept licking his lips. "I sure wish we could play like this all the time. I love this kind of shit."

"Who says we can't?" he looked up at her.

"We can't get into what I like here," she assured him. "I'm a freak, Leroy. The nastiest kind of freak you could imagine."

"I hear you," he said poking her wetness over and over, "but how can I be sure?"

"You can't be sure until you get me out of here," she looked down at him. "We have to leave."

He slid his fingers out of her mound and rubbed his fingers over her nose. "You're good. You almost got me, but I'm older and smarter than you, bitch. Try again."

CHAPTER FIFTEEN

"Pull over right quick, Quita," Theresa said as she sat in the back of Quita's van. "I gotta get something from this store."

Quita was exhausted with Theresa already. All she wanted to do was find Pooh and dump this slut off at the nearest hoe stroll. "Theresa, it's getting late already. We really have to find Pooh to see if she got these kids."

"Oh my, God! I'm telling you that Pooh got them kids," she yelled from the back seat. "I wish you just trust a bitch for a change."

Zaboy was about to say something about her cursing so much until he remembered what they said about him being extra earlier. He really was trying to be a better kid.

"It ain't about trust, Theresa." Quita told her. "It's about two seven year olds out in the world doing God knows what."

"And them same seven year olds won't turn a different color just because we stop at the liquor store right quick. Now you need me, I don't need you. So either pull over and let me run in this store, or find Pooh on your own."

Clarkita sighed. "Quita, just do what she asks. I gotta get the baby a bottle anyway. And I'm sure Hero wants to stretch his legs."

Quita pulled over and let Theresa and her tiny red mini skirt out of her van. When she vanished inside the run down corner store Quita said, "I'm so over this chick."

"I can't stand her either," Essence added. "But for now we gotta deal with her," she hopped out. "Anybody want anything from the store?"

Zaboy was about to give a response but once again he held himself back.

"What about you, Zaboy?" Essence asked him.

He smiled. "I'd like a soda please."

"Which flavor?"

"Red," he responded.

Everyone looked at each other. Red wasn't a flavor but they let him have it. "You got it," Essence smiled walking into the liquor store."

"What do you think is going to happen?" Quita asked Clarkita as she let the dog out and tied him to the door handle so he wouldn't run off.

She sighed. "To be honest, I don't think Pooh will be wherever we're going," Clarkita grabbed Axel and fed him his bottle. "Have you thought about calling Flex back? Maybe he has an update on his end."

"He scares me," Quita said honestly. "I don't want to call him unless I have an answer for him."

Clarkita shook her head and looked at the riff raff hanging around the liquor store. "I got a feeling this woman will be a complete waste of our time. But we have to follow it until the end."

"I hope you're wrong," Quita admitted.

After Baby Axel was fed, Hero shat and Essence returned, Theresa was still nowhere to be found. They were all packed in the van and waiting on her.

"You want me to go in and get her?" Essence asked. "Every minute counts right now."

Quita said, "Yeah because…"

Theresa came out of the store, thirty minutes later holding a bag shaped like liquor along with a stack of small white cups. She climbed into the van and reclaimed her seat.

"Bitch, I'm so sorry!" she said slapping Quita on her back. "I done got in there and got to running my mouth. I forgot all about ya'll being out here." She wagged the liquor bottle at Zaboy who was staring it down. "Get your eyes off of this," she grinned. "Because what's in here will put hair on your chest and make you a man. Stick to that red soda."

"That's rude," Zaboy said out loud.

"What's rude? Me not giving you none of my liquor?"

"If someone is giving you a ride, you should care about their time."

Theresa rotated her head and looked down at the kid in the tight blue coat and hard brown shoes. Any other time Quita would stop him from talking back to adults, but Theresa so deserved this moment.

"What did you say to me?" Theresa asked him.

"Ms. Quita and her friends picked you up, and you're being mean by not being on time," he focused back on the front of the van. "That's all I'm saying."

"Yeah, well, whatever," she said ignoring him.

It took everything in Quita, Essence and Clarkita's power not to laugh. Finally Zaboy had come in on the right timing. Five minutes and two cups of vodka later, they still hadn't arrived at Davie's house.

"Are you sure we going the right way?" Quita asked looking at Theresa from the rearview mirror. "Because we been driving for a minute."

"Hold my cup," Theresa stuffed the cup into Zaboy's hands and pulled on Quita's headrest to pull herself up. "Oh, damn! We going the wrong way," she looked at the road signs. "We should be heading toward Minnesota Avenue."

Quita sighed. "Do you know where he lives or not?"

"I been to this boy's house enough times to get there with my eyes closed. Just head to Minnesota Avenue already like I told you," she snatched the cup from Zaboy and it seemed awfully lighter. "Yeah, this the right way."

Ten minutes later, after they entered a residential area she said, "Slow down, Quita. We coming up on his house now."

Relieved, Quita reduced the speed of her van when suddenly a hole popped up in Quita's passenger window, shattering it completely. Then she began to hear soft thumps along the side of the van.

"What the fuck!" Quita said in a low voice.

"Ain't no what the fuck! These niggas out here is shooting!" Theresa swallowed the liquor in her cup, slid the van's door back and hopped out. Suddenly a gun materialized from her coat and she started blasting off in all directions.

"Quita, get us the fuck out of here!" Clarkita called out from the front seat. "That bitch is crazy!"

Needing no further motivation, Quita pressed her foot on the gas and took off toward the stop sign. She could clearly see Theresa in the middle of the street firing at some dudes from her rearview mirror. She didn't bother to slow down until she was on the highway and miles away from the scene.

"I truly can't believe this day," Quita said to herself. "If somebody tried to tell me it's not wild I might fight them."

Clarkita said, "I'm gonna have to agree with you this time."

Shit was already rough until she pulled up in front of her house and saw Xtisha's banged out BMW, and another car she didn't recognize. Mike's red Lexus was still on the curb.

"Now what the fuck is going on?" Quita asked throwing her van in park.

"We won't know until we go inside will we?" Essence said. "But I got a feeling it ain't good."

The moment Quita opened the front door to her house and saw Pooh, she felt like there really was a Santa Clause. A smile spread across her face and she made a beeline for her daycare center. It was 5:00pm but if she hurried, she could return Cordon to Flex before he did something else he couldn't take back. Then she'd be able to help Kimi and Valencia by convincing Flex not to kill them.

Boy would they have a laugh about this shit later if they survived. Quita shook her head just thinking about the conversations they would share later.

But when she walked into the basement, the TV was on but there was no Cordon or Miranda in sight. She hopped up the stairs, rushed to the living room and approached Pooh. Out of breath she grabbed her by both arms, "Where…are…the…kids?"

"Quita, I don't mean to be rude, but we got another matter more important than some damn kids." Xtisha said from the sidelines.

Just hearing her voice irritated Quita. Xtisha Daye and Barry aka Lil Goose, were standing in her living room, despite the fact that she didn't fuck with either of them. They were banned from her residence and they knew it. So what were they doing there?

Xtisha's long lanky body appeared to float over everyone, as if she was a ghost. Her fingernails were so long and curly, that when she scratched her head, which was littered in tiny short braids, she had to use her knuckles. Each of her nails were painted in the colors of the rainbow, and matched the scarf around her neck. She didn't leave the house a day without some splash of rainbow, although she claimed she wasn't gay.

"What are you doing in my house?" Quita asked both Xtisha and Lil Goose.

Lil Goose, a short fat kid who always wore a red baseball cap over his eyes, busied himself with the iTouch in his hands. He never left the house without it, along with the ear buds that were stuffed in his ears. Quita made a mistake of taking them away from him one day and he screamed so loud, her eardrum popped.

The thing about Lil Goose was this, he had the innocent eyes of an angel. However, when you got to know him better, you'd soon realize he was as close to Satan as Damien from the movie, "*The Omen*".

In fact, outside of him cursing Quita and Kimi out for blood, she threw him out of her center after he acted violently towards Zaboy.

DAYS EARLIER

Quita was upstairs at the time putting Evanka out of her house, a bitch who wanted her money back, when she heard Miranda yell, "Ms. Quita, Lil Goose took his pants down and sat on Zaboy face! They 'bout to fight and everything!"

When Quita got down the stairs, she almost fell back when she saw the scene. Pooh was holding Zaboy who was flailing wild arms and crying. Blood dripped from his arm and one of Zaboy's ugly shoes lay a few feet over from where he stood. Essence kept Goose back but he kicked his bare legs awkwardly in an attempt to get away. Lil Goose's pants were on the floor and he was naked from the waist down.

Quita walked up to Lil Goose and yelled, "What were you doing?! What the fuck is wrong with you? Why you always gotta be starting shit?!"

Goose said, "He tried to give me pink eye!" he was referring to Zaboy. "My mother said if he touched me to make him kiss my ass! So I made him kiss my ass!"

When Quita asked where the blood was coming from too, she was told that Lil Goose tried to stab Zaboy.

PRESENT DAY

For Quita, that was the final straw. She put him out of her program and as far as she knew, Xtisha was dealing with her archrivals up the street at, Little Kids & Happy Mother's Day Care Center. So what were they doing in her house?

"Xtisha, what are you doing here?" Quita asked again. When she looked down she felt Zaboy hiding behind her legs. He was scared of Goose since the last time he saw him, Goose tried to kill him.

"Wait a minute, Xtisha," Quita looked down at him. "Go downstairs, Zaboy."

He didn't move. Instead he pointed at the boy and said, "The Goose".

"Don't worry," Quita told him, "he won't bother you."

"I got him," Essence said walking him downstairs to the daycare center.

Quita focused back on Xtisha and Goose. "Now what did you say?"

"Your assistant crashed into my car," Xtisha pointed at Pooh. "And now you into me for some money."

Quita laughed Xtisha back a few steps. "Listen here, bitch, first of all she doesn't work for me anymore. Second of all, even if she did you wouldn't get a dime from me. Now get the fuck out of my house before I raise up on your ass," Quita opened the door and pushed Xtisha down the steps.

"You gonna pay for that shit!" Xtisha promised snatching her son with her.

"Yeah right, bitch!" Quita slammed the door in her face and walked back toward Pooh. "Where are the kids?"

Pooh was shaking so much she was about to explode. "I...I..."

"You scaring her," Davie said stepping to her side. "She don't know where the kids are." He told them. "Kimi had her watch the kids at the motel. They went to get a soda and never came back."

Quita felt the air exit her lungs. "What do you mean they never came back? How could you lose them? Do you know that the nigga Flex is killing mothafuckas as we speak because we can't find his son? Shit is serious!"

She went to touch Pooh but Pooh passed out on the floor. "Fuck!" Quita screamed stomping in place.

"So let me get this straight," Mike said stepping up. "She took Flex's son and now he's looking for him?"

"Why?" Quita asked seeing the fire in his eyes.

"Because the man has a right to know where his son is."

"You seemed awfully interested in a child who don't belong to you," Quita responded. "Shouldn't you be more interested in Miranda? And her whereabouts?"

Mike backed down and walked over to Vonzella. "I'm worried about them both. I'm just saying that the man Flex should have the information about his son, and I'm going to give it to him." Mike kissed Vonzella and said, "Give me a second. I'll be right back."

Now shit had kicked up to the next level. Quita had to get everyone out of her house she didn't fuck with before Mike told Flex the news about Cordon.

"What is your name?" she asked Davie.

"Davie," he said fanning Pooh trying to wake her up.

"Ya'll need to go see about Theresa." Quita advised.

He frowned. "See about Theresa, why?"

"Because she was busting off on some niggas outside of your house," Quita continued. "We just left from over there."

His body stiffened and he stood straight up. "Are you serious?"

"I wouldn't even play like that," Quita told him.

Davie ran into the kitchen, came back with a cup of water and threw it in Pooh's face. She spit out water, sat up straight and said, "What's going on?" she wiped her eyes.

"Your mother beefing with the Minnesota Avenue niggas again," Davie informed her. "We gotta go before shit get crazy...again."

Both of them zipped out of her house before Quita could rebut. She had another question to ask Pooh, about the room number, but she was gone in a flash.

Quita turned her attention to Vonzella. "Look, we going to find your daughter. But you gotta give me some time. Okay?"

She was so frazzled that all she could do was nod. "I never treated her right," Vonzella said in a low voice. "Now all I want is my baby back."

"And we gonna get her back," Quita informed her. "Trust me." Quita moved toward the kitchen to get the phone.

"What you gonna do now?" Clarkita asked Quita.

"I'm going to do what you suggested before, call Flex. Before that nigga Mike do."

After making a few phone calls, in his car, Mike was finally speaking to the person he wanted. "Yeah, is this Hambone?"

"Who asking?" the person asked.

"This Silver Mike from Northeast. I got some information for Flex."

"What's the word?" Hambone replied.

"You need to tell him that I got some information that might benefit him."

"What should I tell him it's about?"

"His son," he said arrogantly. "But the information is going to cost him."

Cordon and Miranda lie on Mr. Creepy's bed, face up with their wrists tied together. Mr. Creepy came in and out of the room, trying to fix the video camera, but nothing he seemed to do worked. Originally he thought it was broken, until he considered that the battery needed charging.

"How are my two stars?" he said allowing the battery to charge just enough. "I hope you aren't too uncomfortable."

Silence.

He frowned. "So both of you are going to ignore me now?" he looked them over, oblivious to the fact that they wanted to be home. "Because if you ask me, that's pretty damn rude."

"What are you going to do with us?" Cordon asked.

Miranda, on the other hand, seemed to blank out a long time ago. Cordon called her name several times when Mr. Creepy wasn't in the room, and she didn't respond to him.

"We just want to go home," Cordon continued. He tried to plead with him with his eyes.

"If anything I'd think you'd be up for my plan," Mr. Creepy told him adjusting the position the camera's lenses were in.

"Why?" he frowned.

"Because it will give you an opportunity to kiss that pretty little girlfriend of yours," he pointed at Miranda. "I know you always wanted to."

"So you gonna take a picture of us kissing?" Cordon asked not understanding what he wanted from them.

"Well, it will be kissing at first, but after that, I want you guys to get a little more creative. Don't worry, I'm a director and you'll be just fine."

"What movies have you done?" Cordon asked trying to find out Mr. Creepy's plans for them.

"Well, I directed one called, *My First Kiss* and *My First Time* and this one will be called *My First Boyfriend*."

Cordon was even more confused. And if Mr. Creepy would've asked him, he would've told him that his movie names were whack. "After we do the movie, what are you going to do with us then?"

"It depends," Mr. Creepy moved around the room taking some more cords out of the dresser. "On if you have fans or not. And how long it will take to get the shots that I need."

"But, doesn't it take a long time to put the movie on DVD?" Cordon continued his line of questioning.

Mr. Creepy laughed so hard, his stomach jiggled. "Here it was, I thought I was the old one around here," he slapped his knee. "No, no, no, young man. I can make the transfer to DVD later. First you guys are going to go live in front of an audience, where people will pay me to see you."

Cordon's stomach swirled.

"I'll be right back," Mr. Creepy said leaving the room again.

When they were alone, Cordon stared at the ceiling. What he wouldn't give to see his father Flex again. Cordon wondered was his father looking for him. A smile spread across his face when he felt in his heart that he was. Although Flex could be rough with other people, Cordon knew for a fact that he loved him. Now something in the pit of his stomach told him that he'd never see his father again.

"He's going to make us do the nasty," Miranda advised Cordon. "And stuff like that."

Cordon turned his head in her direction. Now he was staring into her pretty face. "What's that?"

She frowned. "You never heard of it?"

Cordon felt dumb.

"He's going to make us kiss and touch each other," she schooled him.

Cordon was horrified. He wasn't old enough to do any of those things. But the bigger question was, how did she know? "He didn't say that. He said we were making a movie and that people would be watching."

Miranda laughed at him. "The ones who like the tapes, and stuff like that too, be on them," she looked at the ceiling. "To watch it for later."

"You ever make a movie before?" Cordon interrogated.

"I've made some," she shrugged. "I hated them all though. I was never smiling in any of them when they made me watch."

He swallowed. "Who were you in the movie with?"

"My uncles," she advised him as if it were natural. "I haven't been in a movie with uncle Mike, but he likes to kiss me. He's not hard like the other ones though. He does it really soft."

Suddenly Cordon wanted to find this Uncle Mike and punch him in the face. "Isn't your uncle, like your family and stuff? That's nasty."

"None of my uncles are family," She shook her head. "I guess that's what makes it okay. They be my mother's boyfriends. She have a new one every other month it seems. But I hate all of them. And sometimes I hate her, too," a tear rolled down her face and dampened the pillow. "But I want to see her now though," she looked at Cordon. "Even if it's for a little bit."

"I'm sorry, that you had to do stuff you didn't want to with them dudes," Cordon said softly.

She sighed. "Well at least this time I like the person I'm gonna be in the movie with," she smiled. "A lot."

Cordon' stomach rumbled. Yes he thought it would be cool to kiss a girl. But he wasn't in the business of kissing a girl who was forced to kiss him back. Just the thought gave him power. He had to get her out of there. Miranda had been through enough and he wasn't about to put her through more.

"Let's scoot to the edge of the bed," Cordon announced.

Miranda looked at the open door. "He's gonna come back and hurt us," she said shaking her head back and forth.

"Miranda, this man is going to make you do stuff you don't want to. If you wanna leave, we have to do something to stop him. Okay?"

She nodded.

"Good, now let's move to the edge of the bed," he commanded.

They quickly scooted to the edge of the bed. "When he comes back, I'm going to hit him with my free hand," Cordon quarterbacked. "I'm going to hit him as hard as I can. You stay out of the way. So you don't get hurt. Okay?"

She nodded. "Okay," Miranda mumbled.

They sat quietly on the edge of the bed and waited for Mr. Creepy to reenter. A few minutes later, he did.

"What's going on with you two?" he asked sitting two glasses of orange juice, with a powdery cloud in both of them, on the dresser. "Is the bed not comfortable enough?"

No one responded. Cordon was breathing hard, trying to dig up the strength to go for what he knew. But for some reason, Mr. Creepy looked larger than he appeared when he first saw him. Now he was doubting his plan and himself. But when he looked over at Miranda, who was visibly shaken, he got the strength to charged the man at full speed.

Cordon's head dove into the pit of the man's stomach. On impact, Mr. Creepy gripped Cordon by his left underarm and swung him toward the dresser. The edge of the dresser attacked the middle of Cordon's back, causing him severe pain. Since Miranda was connected to him, she was thrown around too. Although the pain was enough, it didn't stop Cordon's plight.

Cordon threw blow after blow on the man's leg, stomach and thighs. But Mr. Creepy was maneuvering Cordon and Miranda like they were as light as pillows. Until something happened.

Miranda snapped.

Although some people who knew Miranda wrote her off as sneaky, and didn't want the nosey girl roaming around their house, if she would've gotten proper help it would have been determined that something else was going on in her mind. She'd been taken advantage of most of her young life and it caused her to act out in crazy ways.

For starters Miranda was a fighter who would bite chunks out of your skin if you got in her way or tried to harm her. That very trait was why some of Vonzella's boyfriends didn't get an opportunity to touch her.

The thing which most people didn't realize, was despite her violent nature, she had an above average intelligence. The school board said that she would be as close to a genius as a kid could get, if she could get her behavior under control. Now Miranda was using her violent nature to her advantage.

Once Miranda was on her feet, she chewed into the old man's thigh like it was a rib eye steak. The pain immediately hit him because he suffered from muscular issues every day of his life. This was the worst thing that could be happening for Mr. Creepy, because most of his agony was in the leg she chose to attack. The soreness he experienced by her strong teeth, weakened his strength and stuttered his movements.

"I won't let you hurt me again!" Miranda screamed in between gnawing. "You won't!"

Cordon stood back hoping not to get bitten in her rage.

"I never touched you!" Mr. Creepy yelled trying to pull her off of his leg. He wasn't having any such luck because Miranda was quick like a rabid dog. "Stop it!"

Miranda went to work so good on Mr. Creepy, that he grabbed both of them by the necks and tossed them both into the night. They rolled down the stairs and Cordon bumped his head on the last one.

"Stay away from my house!" Mr. Creepy yelled slamming the door in their faces.

On his feet, Cordon was able to get the rope off of their wrists and both of them took off running up the street. They didn't stop until they were five blocks away from the house.

Out of breath, Cordon slumped on the ground and leaned up against a fence. Miranda sat on the ground with him. Nothing but the sounds of their heavy breaths were heard.

Although Miranda was relieved they were safely away, Cordon was angry. He was annoyed that she didn't listen to him when he said he didn't want to enter the house. He was annoyed that he allowed her to get into his head, and have him leave his babysitter, Pooh. He was annoyed they were outside again, and it was nighttime. He couldn't take much of the drama anymore.

Cordon leaped up and started walking quickly down the street.

Miranda jumped up and followed behind him. "Cordon, are you mad at me?"

Silence.

"Cordon!" Miranda continued to scream. "Did I do something wrong?"

He stopped walking and looked at her. "I told you I didn't want to go into the house. I told you I didn't want to go," he repeated. "But you didn't want to listen to me! Now look what happened!"

"But I wanted to..."

"It doesn't matter," he started walking away from her again but she wasn't chasing him anymore. Instead she was crying.

When he turned around and walked back up to her, he felt guilty. Now he really screwed up. "I'm sorry, Miranda."

"No you not," she sobbed hitting his arm. "You hate me! And I hate myself too."

"I don't hate you," he said rubbing his arm to rid the pain. "You just gotta listen to me. Or else I can't be your boyfriend no more."

Her eyes widened. "You're my boyfriend?"

"If I am, I'm not going to be it anymore if you don't listen to me."

She wiped her tears. "Okay, I'm sorry. I just want to go home." After being outside for some time she realized how cold she was. "It's getting scarier out here."

"I want to go home too," Cordon admitted. "When you were back there, you said nobody would hurt you anymore. What did you mean?" Cordon questioned.

Silence.

Miranda observed him. It was obvious that she wished she hadn't shared that information with him. "I just really want to go home," she told him. "Okay?"

"Do you know how much time I've spent on you?" Flex asked Kimi, who was in and out of consciousness. "A day and a half now. It's longer than any parent should deal with a missing child. If you wanted to hurt me, Kimi, you done that."

Kimi shook her head slowly. "I'm sorry that this isn't important enough for you to allow me some of your time."

"You know what I mean, Kimi," Flex sat on the edge of the bed and looked up at her. "Aren't you tired of this yet? Don't you want peace of mind?"

She laughed. "To be honest, I don't even feel that much pain anymore," she giggled. When she observed her surroundings she saw the room was ransacked. "I guess you couldn't find anything in here about him could you?"

"This is funny to you. Isn't it?"

"I'm not laughing at you," Kimi said softly. "But I'm good about all the decisions I make. Because I don't have anything else to worry about. In a while, I'll be able to put all of this behind me. I'm dying," she smiled as if she'd just won the lottery.

"If you wanted to kill yourself, did you have to use me?" he asked angrily.

She laughed again. "No, but you doing it for me is a bonus," she smiled wider. "Come closer."

"Kimi, I don't feel like this shit right now. I want to know where my fucking son is. Stop playing with me."

"So a dying lady asks for one wish, and you're not going to give it to her?"

"Why do you keep talking like this is the end? All you have to do is tell me where Cordon is. When you do, we can get you some help and everybody can get on with the rest of their lives."

"Where is Valencia?" Kimi inquired lowering her brow.

He sighed. "Why?"

"Because I want to know."

"She's at Tech's house," Flex sighed and looked out ahead. "Everything and everybody is being held up pending what you have to tell me," he focused on her. "So you see, Kimi, you have everybody's life in your hands. You got all the power."

"Well I never wanted all the power," Kimi said softly thinking about Quita. "Is Quita okay?"

"For now," he threatened.

She sighed. "You know, all I ever wanted was my Jamie."

Flex squinted. "Who the fuck is Jamie?"

"That's what I called my baby, in my mind anyway," she moved a little to get comfortable. "But Cordon will never hear me call him that."

"Kimi, I've told you everything I can for you to tell me where our son is. You're making this matter final when it doesn't have to be the case."

"That's just it. You've *told* me everything I wanted to hear," Kimi laughed. "You're telling me anything you can, to get me to tell you where my son is. But you don't mean any of it. Do you?"

Flex swallowed at his oversight. "My word is all I have to give you right now, Kimi. Like I've said, you hold all the cards. Not me."

"Well, since I hold all the cards, I want to make two phone calls. One to my mother, and the other to Valencia."

"You know I can't let you call your mother," Flex said in a deep voice. "I can't risk you telling her something, and her calling the police." He was uneasy with her requests.

"Well let me call Valencia and Quita. It's not like they don't know what's going on anyway."

Flex didn't appreciate the shenanigans. But his hands were tied at the moment. So he pulled out his cellphone and called Quita's number. She didn't answer the phone. "I guess she's not there."

Kimi seemed disappointed. "Okay, can you call Valencia?"

Flex dialed the number of the last call he received from Leroy. When the phone rang, he handed it to her. "Here. Make it quick."

Kimi took the phone and said, "Can I speak to Valencia?"

"Who's this?" Leroy asked.

Kimi was short on energy and wanted to reserve some of it so she said to Flex, "Can you please get him to put her on the phone?"

Flex snatched the phone and said, "Look, put the bitch on the phone," he handed it back to Kimi without waiting on Leroy's response.

"Really classy," Kimi said to Flex shaking her head.

A second later Valencia got on the phone. "Hello."

"Valencia, it's Kimi," she whispered.

"Kimi, what the fuck is going on?!" Valencia screamed into the handset. Flex could hear her voice clearly from where he sat. "Do you have Cordon? If so please give him back. These niggas are going to kill me!"

"Listen to me," Kimi said softly, "because I'm kind of weak right now."

Valencia seemed annoyed and anxious. "What's up?"

"I just wanted to tell you that you're one of the worst bitches that I've ever met before in my life. And that Quita made a second rate move by letting you into her life. She should've never hitched her star to your wagon."

"Kimi, I don't have time for this shit. Now do you know where his son is or not?"

"Listen to me, Valencia," Kimi said regaining control. "If I die, my only happiness is that when this shit is all said and done, I know that at least they took care of your scandalous ass."

"Fuck you!" Valencia screamed.

"Too late. You already did that," Kimi ended the call and handed the phone back to Flex. "Thank you. I feel better already."

"Real classy," he said shaking his head. He stuffed his cell phone back into his pocket.

"Well, what can I say?" she shrugged. "I learned from the best."

Flex looked at the clock on the wall and sighed. "We're out of time now, Kimi. So what do you want to do?"

She took a few moments before answering. She thought about her life and she thought about her mother. A smile came to her face when she remembered all the great things her mother had done for her. Sure she lied about what happened to her baby, when she told her mother that she had a miscarriage. But she figured her mother's life was so full, that she didn't want to burden her with her truths. She only hoped that she made her proud, even if her life was just a lie.

"Kimi, what are you going to do?" Flex repeated.

"Tell my son I…"

Her sentence couldn't be finished because Flex placed the barrel to her head and pulled the trigger. Red jelly-like blood and brain matter splashed out of her head and slapped against the walls behind her. He was done with her. Tired of fucking around.

The thing was, the moment Flex pulled the trigger, he realized he made a mistake. As evident as it was, that Kimi would not tell him anything about Cordon, she was his last hope. He was getting ready to make his next move when his phone rang.

He removed it from his pocket and answered. "Flex, this is Barry. You got a minute?"

"I can't make any moves right now, my man," Flex told him, referring to dropping off the coke pack he bought a few days ago. "I got a situation I gotta round up and then I'll get up with you."

"This ain't about that," Barry responded.

"Well what do you want?" Flex walked toward the door.

"Some nigga name Silver Mike called. He told me to tell you he had some information on your boy. Said some bitch name Quita was holding out on you, and to meet him at her house."

Flex could see his heart moving in his chest. Here it was, he trusted Quita and she knew where his son was the entire time? He felt like a fool.

"What else he say?" Flex said trying to hold down his anger.

"He said that the info's gonna cost you."

CHAPTER EIGHTEEN

"Zaboy, why would you do that?" Quita asked holding his drunken body in her arms downstairs in the daycare center. "You weren't supposed to be drinking any liquor. You're just a child!"

Zaboy's smile was eerie and exceptionally wide. "Cuz," he burped and farted at the same time, "I want to be a man. And the lady said the stuff in the cup will put hair on my chest," he lifted his shirt. "Do I got any yet?"

"Zaboy, you are going to get into a lot of trouble now," Quita warned him. "A whole lot of trouble."

"But you said once I be a man," he burped, "that I can get in grown folks talks now. Can I?"

Quita sat him down on the bed and stood up. She walked over to Clarkita and Essence who were observing the entire scene.

"Cruella is going to murder me when she comes here and sees her kid like that," Quita said covering her mouth. "I don't have time for this shit," she whispered. "Not to mention the fact that I have a house full of unwanted visitors upstairs."

"What time does Cruella get here?" Clarkita asked holding Baby Axel in her arm while Hero licked his foot. "Maybe we can get some coffee into him or something."

Quita looked at her watch, "In about an hour."

Essence said, "I got a plan." She rushed to her purse and took out her cell phone. Then she dialed a number and waited. Seconds later she said, "Cruella, you wouldn't believe what happened today. Well you know I'm in college right?" she paused again. "Well I took

Zaboy to a talent show at my school. It's for a fundraiser and guess what girl," she paused, "he won! They done gave him some money and everything." she paused. "Yes, girl he really is that good." she winked at Quita and Clarkita.

"I knew you would be excited. But there's one thing, there's another competition in about an hour. I wanted him to enter that one too but if he does, we won't get back until about 10:00 tonight. Now I can take him back to Quita's if you want me to," she paused. "And we can call the entire thing off." Essence paused again. "Perfect! I'll call you when we make it to Quita's." She ended the call and walked back over to them.

"It worked?" Quita asked.

"Yep," Essence nodded proud of her work. "And she told me to tell you that her son was talented after all."

When the phone rang again Essence took it out of her purse and answered it. "Hello," she paused and her eyes widened in horror. "You can't speak to him now."

Quita felt like she was about to have a baby. She knew it wouldn't work.

"Because he's in the line to get on stage right now," Essence continued. "I know you want to wish him luck but…you know what, on second thought, let me pull him out of the competition," Essence said as if she really were. "Because it's obvious this won't work. There are some talent scouts down here too but I guess he will never benefit." Essence paused. There was a long period of silence before she said, "Perfect. I'll let you know how he does," she ended the call and threw her phone back in her purse.

Everyone exhaled.

Quita rolled her eyes. "That was a close ass call," she looked at Zaboy. "But what are we going to do about him?" she pointed at Zaboy who was staring at them with glassy eyes. "You know that boy gonna tell Cruella everything when she finally gets him tonight."

"Not if I warn him that he'll be in trouble for having grown people's juice," Essence responded. "Don't worry about it, Quita. You have enough shit on your plate. I'll work on Zaboy," she looked at him. "I'll work on him real good."

"How did you learn to lie so well?" Clarkita asked Essence. "You're at pro level if you ask me."

"I hope you're right," Essence giggled. "Because I'm going to school for law," she grinned. "I guess I'm supposed to be a good liar."

The three of them laughed a little and it was the first time all day. It wasn't long before Quita sighed, "Okay, but what about them upstairs?" she looked at Cruella and Essence.

"That's where you come in," Essence admitted. "Because I did my part."

And she was right.

Quita and Clarkita walked up the stairs to see Mike and Vonzella talking amongst themselves across the living room. Essence remained downstairs with Zaboy, the baby and the dog. Quita and Clarkita stopped in the kitchen and observed them.

"You can leave anytime you want," Quita told Clarkita, "because with all the sneaky talking that them two are doing, I feel an ambush coming along," she looked at her.

Clarkita waved Quita off. "Listen, I done slapped a kid who isn't mine, been in the car while a shoot out was going down and I'm a witness to a kidnapping and hostage situation," she looked into Quita's eyes, "Truth be told, I haven't had this much fun in years."

Quita laughed but felt warm inside. Clarkita was a soldier. But why? At the end of the day, Quita felt she didn't deserve this type of loyalty. Clarkita was starting to be a better friend to her than both Valencia and Kimi put together. Quita looked up to her like a mother, and she could really use her strength at a time like this.

"You must have a background you haven't told me about yet," Quita responded.

"Let's just say I grew up in a family of gang members," she sighed. "So to tell you the truth, there ain't much that I haven't seen. This is simply a refresher."

"I'm learning more and more about the doctor everyday," Quita admitted.

"If we end up being friends long enough, you haven't seen anything yet," Clarkita stated.

"Let me handle this shit," Quita said. They both walked over to Vonzella and Mike.

"Any word on my daughter yet?" Vonzella asked Quita.

"No," Quita responded, "I'm waiting on Pooh to pick up the phone, so she can tell us which motel she went to along with the room number. I called her a rack of times. She got out of here so fast that I didn't get a chance to ask her."

"Are you sure you're telling the truth?" Mike questioned Quita. "After all, you did lie about knowing what was going on before. What changed now?"

"Because you know everything," Quita told him. "And there ain't no need in lying no more."

"Why would Pooh do this?" Vonzella interrupted. "It just doesn't make any sense to me."

Quita didn't want to tell Vonzella the truth. Besides, the real story was too long and drawn out. At the end of the day, the only ties Miranda had to the entire situation was that Cordon was sweet on her. And to calm him down, Kimi needed Miranda. Other then that, Miranda would not be involved.

"People do dumb things." Clarkita said rubbing Vonzella's arm. "But I have faith that we are going to find both of them, and they'll be fine. I know it's hard but try not to worry yourself so much."

"Fuck faith," Mike said eyes glued on Clarkita. For whatever reason, he looked like he hated her.

Everyone's head swiveled in his direction. "Why would you say something so crass?" Clarkita questioned. "Even if that's how you felt, to shit on everyone else's belief's is tasteless."

It was evident that Mike was slightly embarrassed at how Clarkita went at him. "Just like you have your belief's, I have mine. And I say faith don't have shit to do with this. This is about money and greed. Let's call it like it is."

"I feel sorry for you, young man," Clarkita looked deeply into his eyes. "I see some dark things in you, and I pray to God I'm not right."

Mike laughed although the older woman gave him the spooks. "People kill me with that line." He shook his head. *"I feel sorry for you young man"*, he mocked her. Always getting mad when a nigga don't agree with you. Listen here lady, I don't need no prayer and I don't need nobody feeling sorry for me. I'm good over here."

"Not for long," Clarkita said stepping back. "I already see how shit is going down for you."

"Hold up," Mike walked in Clarkita's direction. "So you threatening me?"

"Mike, what are you doing?" Vonzella asked. "That's an older woman," she went to pull him back but was paid for her efforts with an elbow to the face. Her chin split open and bled.

Quita was right about him all along. He was abusing her.

"What I tell you about talking when I'm not pointing at you?"

Vonzella didn't respond. "I said what the fuck did I tell you about that shit, bitch?"

"You said not to do it," Vonzella replied weakly holding her hand over her wound to stop the blood flow.

"Then don't do it again!" Mike said pointing down at her head.

When Mike turned around, the tip of a Wusthof kitchen knife was grazing his chin. And Clarkita was its operator.

Mike didn't move. Instead, he raised his arms up in surrender. "What…are…you…doing…old…lady?"

"Please don't kill him," Vonzella begged her with smeared blood all over her face and fingers. "He didn't mean to do it. He just don't know his own strength."

Clarkita felt pity and anger for the woman. She focused back on Mike. "I watched a man your age when I was a kid, beat my mother to death. I'm talking about he really killed her. With his own hands he took away her life leaving us motherless and alone.

Since that time, I done told every man I come in contact with two things. Number one, that I'm not the girl to be hit. And number two, I will never stand by and watch a woman be beat in my presence again, and do nothing," she looked him square in the eyes. "I don't know, son, but I'm feeling the world might be better off without you."

"Listen," Mike spoke softly, "if you don't get that knife out of my face in one minute, I'm gonna hurt you. And it's gonna be bad."

Clarkita was about to carve up his face like a pumpkin until Quita grabbed her. "Don't do this," Quita begged her. "Your baby is downstairs and he needs you." When Clarkita didn't respond Quita said, "And I need you. Please."

Clarkita was breathing so heavily, that her chest rose and fell repeatedly. She lowered the knife and backed away from Mike. "You gonna get yours," she vowed pointing at him. "I feel it."

"I'm gonna get you for that shit," Mike said. "I'm gonna see you in the streets and when I do, its gonna be over."

"Until we meet again," Clarkita told him.

Quita was still referring the possible fight between Clarkita and Mike, until her house phone rang. She quickly answered and was relieved when it was Pooh.

"Do you know where Kimi is?" Pooh asked.

"No," Quita lied. "But, Pooh, I need the motel where you were at with the kids."

"Oh," Pooh sang into the phone. "I forgot to tell you where the motel was. It's just that my mother almost died in that shoot out and…"

"Pooh, not for nothing, but I'm not even interested in Theresa right now," Quita said observing Clarkita and Mike giving each other dagger eyes across the living room. "Where is the motel?"

Pooh gave her the information and Quita wrote it all down and hung up. She was about to go to the motel, but there was a knock at the door. When Mike opened it,

Flex and Morton walked inside. Flex's eyes looked as if he hadn't slept in days and hair stubble peaked out along his face.

Flex walked directly up to Mike. "Are you the nigga they call Silver Mike?"

Mike puffed out his chest and said, "Yeah," he pointed at himself for effect. "That's me."

Flex grinned. "So I'm in the right place.

Mike was too stupid to know that he was in trouble. "You sure are. I see you got the message."

"I did," Flex nodded. "Now you said you have some information on my boy," he looked around. "So where is he?"

"This bitch over there," Mike pointed at Quita, "found out that your son was at a motel with some bitch name Pooh."

Flex scratched his head remembering hearing the name earlier from Quita.

"She wasn't trying to tell you that info," Mike continued. "So I'm letting you know."

"Is he here now?" Flex asked unimpressed.

"No, but I'm sure with that information you can find him now," Mike looked at Vonzella's bloodied face. "This here is Vonzella. She's Miranda's mother. Your son is somewhere out there with her daughter."

Flex remembered her name. It was all Cordon could talk about when he last saw him. It was Miranda this and Miranda that. If the little girl was anything as beautiful as her mother, Flex could see why he was wired up.

"Looks to me like you know how to treat the ladies," Flex said referring to Vonzella's bloodied face. "But it seems to me like we still have a problem." Flex stepped closer to Mike. "So let me get this straight before I go any further, are you telling me that you don't have any useful information for me."

Mike swallowed hard. "Yeah man I just..."

Morton shot Mike so quickly in the middle of his forehead, that no one but Flex knew what happened.

Vonzella screamed her lungs out witnessing her boyfriend take the fall. She dropped to her knees and picked up his head. She was hysterical and making a lot of extra noise until Morton aimed at her.

"Not yet," Flex told Morton. He lowered the gun.

Vonzella was the mother of his son's girlfriend so he would try to give her a pass. Flex looked a Vonzella and said, "I'm going to need you to calm down." When her whimpering grew louder Flex said, "If you don't I will kill you. Okay?"

She was still trembling but this time she placed her bloody hands over her mouth and softened her cries. They were barely audible now.

"Good, girl." Flex turned around to Clarkita and Quita who were stuck. "Why didn't you tell me about the motel, Quita."

Quita raised the paper in her hand that she'd written Pooh's notes on. "We just found out the address before you walked in, Flex. I didn't want to end up like Mike by giving you information that didn't lead to anything," Quita continued hoping Flex would believe her.

Flex rubbed his head. "This is the worst fucking day of my life." He looked at Mike's corpse and scratched his head. "Is your center still open? I mean, are kids here right now?"

"Yes," Quita nodded.

"Morton, take the nigga's body to the trunk. I don't want no kids seeing this shit," Flex looked back at Quita. "What's the address to the motel?"

Quita handed it to him. "Apparently they were with Pooh, Kimi's cousin," Quita advised. "And for whatever reason, both of the kids left the room."

Flex seemed defeated. "Pooh didn't say why? I mean, if she was supposed to be watching them they should've never left her sight."

"She's irresponsible, Flex. That's why I had to fire her."

Flex sighed. "Well let's go to the motel and see if Cordon's there now. Because if I don't find my kid within the next few hours, I don't know who I might kill next.

CHAPTER NINETEEN

Valencia was sitting on the edge of Tech's bed, with Leroy. She was still mad at Kimi's call. "I can't believe that bitch played me half like that," Valencia continued. "After all the shit I did for her."

While Valencia's thoughts were with Kimi, Leroy was in her ear asking what his son said. "Are you sure he didn't ask about me?"

Valencia sighed. "Leroy, I told you everything that happened when she got on the phone. The call was about me and my ex-best friend."

The only good thing that came from the call was that now Leroy seemed uninterested in her, and more interested in what was on Flex's mind.

"But why did he sound like he was so mad at me?" Leroy continued. "When he told me to hand you the phone."

Valencia sighed. "I told you but you're not listening," Valencia looked at him. "He knows you raped his wife and he's going to take care of you. I been trying to tell you that all day."

"If Flex is so mad at me," Leroy started, "then why didn't he say that when I spoke to him earlier?"

Valencia was beyond annoyed with the old man. "Well what exactly did Flex say would happen when he came back here?" she looked into his eyes.

Leroy played the tapes back in his mind and said; "He said something about giving me what's coming to me, or what I deserve."

Valencia laughed. "And that makes you think shit is sweet between you two?" she shook her head. "You really are delusional, Leroy. The man has made clear what he's going to do to you. How much more proof do you need?"

Leroy got out of the bed and walked to the window. He looked out of it. "I don't know what to do now."

"Maybe I can help you come up with some ideas," Valencia said in a low voice. "Seems to me that we're in the same predicament."

"Not necessarily," Leroy responded not wanting to face the truth. That he was un-benefit as far as Flex was concerned. "You have ropes on your wrists, I don't."

"You so blind you can't see," Valencia grinned. "You have invisible ropes on too and the longer you stay here, the tighter they get. Because once he finds his son, he's coming back to clear up loose ends."

Leroy turned from the window to look at her. "If I was going to go along with you, what is your plan?"

"Well, first you have to take this shit off my arms," she raised her wrists so that he could focus on the ropes.

Leroy frowned at them. "And then what?"

"And then you go in there and take care of Maine," she whispered. "I heard him go to the bathroom earlier, when I was on the phone with Kimi. I wouldn't be surprised if he isn't up to something right now."

Leroy's eyebrows rose. "That nigga can't do shit but babysit his dick," he giggled. "You told me you bit down on his hardware. The last thing he thinking about is me and you. Plus I checked on him a little while ago and he was snoring."

"Well maybe he put some ice on his balls or something," Valencia shrugged. "Because I could've sworn I heard the nigga moving in the living room. And you know he's mad."

"If he's mad at anybody it's you," he said waving the gun at her. "You're the one who feasted on him. Not me."

"But he asked you for the gun back. And you wouldn't give it to him. Told the nigga he already had his hands full and everything. You don't think he's salty about that shit?"

"Even if he is, in his condition he can't do shit about it."

"Why are you afraid to kill him?" Valencia questioned tilting her head. "This is not a game. I predict that Flex is going to kill Kimi and find his son at any minute. If he doesn't have him now. If I know Kimi, she probably has Pooh holding Cordon or some shit like that," she continued. "Anyway, once Flex kills Kimi, and finds whoever has his kid, he's coming here to take care of you. We don't have a lot of time, Leroy. Let's move now!"

"Fuck," Leroy said under his breath looking down at the floor. "Just so you know, wherever I go you coming with me," Leroy advised her.

Whether he knew it or not, she had no intentions of staying with his pussy snatching ass. But instead of telling him that she said, "I'm all yours," Valencia produced a smile. "Besides, we a team now!"

CHAPTER TWENTY

Cordon and Miranda lucked up on a playground in the middle of a large park. They were sitting on swings in the pitch of the night. Miranda's cough worsened due to the frigid temperatures. They wanted to ask for help, but everybody around them seemed scary. And after meeting Mr. Creepy, the last thing they wanted was to appear vulnerable to the wrong person again.

"If you could eat anything in the world right now," Miranda asked coughing softly, "what would it be?"

Cordon smiled. "I'd have a big piece of pizza and some ketchup french fries," he looked up at the stars. "Oh, and some chocolate ice cream, too."

"You love chocolate ice cream don't you?" she asked swinging slowly, with her feet planted in the dead leaves. The squeaky sound of the swing played in the background.

"My mother use to make it for me," Cordon smiled. "It was homemade and my favorite." he looked up at the sky again. "She was going to open an ice cream shop before she died," he sighed.

"I didn't like chocolate ice cream before I met you," Miranda admitted. "But it's good now," she coughed again.

Cordon couldn't believe his ears. "If you could eat anything in the world, what would it be?"

Miranda grinned. "Popcorn, a Snickers and a red soda," she swung a little harder and her feet lifted off the ground. "I like to pour red soda over my popcorn. And watch it turn colors and stuff."

Cordon frowned. "That sounds nasty.

"No it's not. I use to eat it with my grandmother all the time before she died," Miranda sighed. She looked at him seriously, "Cordon, what are we going to do?"

"I don't know yet," he groaned. "I'm still thinking."

"But its getting later," she coughed three times and held her chest. "Are you mad at me, for making you leave the motel?"

"I was, but not anymore," he said although he wasn't sure.

"Why not?"

"Because if you saw something wrong, then maybe it was a good idea that we left," he hunched his shoulders. "I don't know."

"I'm hungry, Cordon. I didn't want to say anything, because I didn't want to think about it, but it's getting bad now. I haven't had anything to eat since yesterday."

"Me either," he recalled not wanting to focus on the rotten bananas he was forced to eat.

She coughed again. "So what can we do?"

"There is a store across the street," he pointed at it. They'd been watching people enter and leave the whole time, trying to determine whom they could trust. "I'm going to get you something."

Miranda's eyes widened and sparkled under the moon's light. "But how? You don't have no money. You left it back at the motel. In your coat."

"I'm going to take it," he said looking at her. "I don't know."

"But that's not honest," Miranda said in a low voice.

"I don't know what else to do," he confessed. "And I'm hungry too."

They both looked across the street. "What we gonna do after that?"

Miranda was putting a lot of pressure on him, but he was going to try his best to be strong. "I think we should go back to the motel."

"But I don't trust Miss Pooh."

"I'm not talking about going to her," he said swinging softly. "I think we should see the lady with the long braids. The one who said we are cute together. In the hallway."

"Oh..." Miranda said nodding, "She was nice. And real pretty."

"Maybe if we go back to the motel, we can ask to use her phone. She might let us."

Miranda grinned considering the possibilities. "I wish we would've thought about the lady first. Maybe we would not have met Mr. Creepy."

"I know," Cordon got off the swing. "But let's not think about him anymore. That man made me mad. And I'm gonna tell my pops the first time I see him too."

"What you think he gonna do?" she asked getting off the swing also.

"I don't know," he said shaking his head. "But I don't think it will be nice."

Cordon went down the aisles within the store looking for popcorn. Before he went inside, he asked Miranda what flavor she liked the most. She said the original and that was what he was going for.

When he saw blue shiny bags of popcorn, he looked around. No one was within his sights so he stuffed it under his shirt making his figure bigger than it was before he came in. With one item off the list, he strolled to the candy aisle. He observed the scene again. There was a couple on the far end of the store, but they weren't looking at him. So he stuffed a Snickers bar in his pocket.

He grabbed a few Twix bars for himself and was about to leave. He looked around again, and it looked as if the coast was clear. Cordon was about to walk out, when out of his peripheral vision, he saw a white large man walking quickly in his direction. His heart thumped in his chest wildly. He was going to be caught and possibly arrested. His worst fear. He over heard his father speaking of the times he spent in jail, and didn't want to go that route. But when the man passed him, and walked out of the store, Cordon breathed a sigh of relief.

From where he stood in the store, he could see Miranda. She looked worried. When he pointed at his shirt, she smiled at him and he couldn't help but smile also.

Cordon walked quicker toward her, until suddenly something was wrong. A heavy hand rested on his shoulder and pulled him back. One minute he was about to be near Miranda, and the next he was far away from her. The popcorn and candy he'd stolen fell out of his shirt and slapped against the grungy floor. The man picked the stolen items up and continued to pull Cordon towards the back.

Miranda ran inside but Cordon shook his head rapidly from left to right. She didn't know what that meant but it didn't matter anyway. Because in a second, Cordon was pulled inside an office and the door was shut.

Once inside, Cordon was thrown into a chair. A heavyset white man, with a walkie-talkie looked at him. Then he hit a button on the walkie-talkie, "I have the kid in my custody, I'm waiting on you." he placed the large gray receiver on top of the table.

Cordon was beyond embarrassed that he'd been caught. In his mind he couldn't do anything right for his new girlfriend. He bet money that she wouldn't want to have anything to do with him now.

"Why were you in my store stealing?" the man finally asked. It was then that Cordon noticed that he had piercing blue eyes. "You look too young to be doing something like this. Did somebody put you up to it?"

Before Cordon could respond, an older black woman with a serious frown walked inside. She was all business and no play until she looked at Cordon's face. "Oh my goodness," she looked at the white man. "He's just a child."

She sat next to Cordon. "Where are your parents, young man?"

Silence.

"Baby, where are your people?" she asked again.

"Are you stealing because you're hungry?" the man questioned Cordon. "Because if you are, all you have to do is tell us now," he observed the fact that he didn't have a jacket on. "And where is your coat? It's freezing outside."

Before giving them an answer, Cordon remembered what his father always said, *'Son, before giving a response to any inquiry, consider the question.'* So Cordon thought about why they were asking was he hungry or who put him up to it. He didn't want anybody looking down on his father and he certainly didn't want Miranda being drug inside the creepy room.

Instead of playing into their hand, Cordon said what he heard his father say before, "I want a lawyer."

The woman looked at the other officer. "Did you just say you want a lawyer?"

Cordon looked her dead into her eyes. "Yeah. Don't kids got rights too?"

She shook her head and stood up. "I don't know what's going on with you, but you're making this harder than it has to be, young man. I'm not the enemy. I really want to help you."

"And if you knew her, you'd know that virtually never happens." The white man chimed in.

"I want a lawyer," Cordon repeated.

She sighed. "Are you here with anyone?"

Cordon thought about Miranda. "No. I'm by myself."

"This is so sad," she said moving to the door. "I've been at this store for twenty seven years, and this is the first time I want to stop a shoplifter from going to jail, but he doesn't want my help," she sighed. "I guess you live and learn."

"It happens to the best of us," the male officer said.

"Well son, since you don't want our help, you'll have to be transported to the precinct. What is your parent's number?"

"I want my lawyer first."

Irritated she opened the door and said, "Get the cops down here, Bob. Let's see how much lawyer talk he'll be saying then."

Seven-year-old Cordon was walked out of the office. The first person he saw was Miranda. She was about to approach him but he shook his head and yelled out, "Go to the motel!"

"What you talking about boy?" the officer said. When he looked around the store, he saw a bunch of people and Miranda standing next to a man like he was her father. She was as smart as a whip.

"See," Cordon said trying to bring attention back on himself. "I ain't talking to nobody. I want my…"

"Lawyer," he said in a hefty voice. "You told me that already."

Cordon felt bad for leaving Miranda by herself, but the last thing he wanted was her to be arrested. When he approached the police car, the man opened the door and put him inside. The outside officer spoke to two other policemen, who stepped out of the cruiser.

From the inside, Cordon could hear them but he was focused on Miranda inside the store. She stood next to the magazine stand and she was waving at him. He only hoped he was making the best decision at the moment by leaving her alone.

A few minutes later, two officers climbed inside the cruiser. "So I understand you want a lawyer huh?" A young black officer said turning on the engine.

"Getting started in crime early, huh?" the other asked as he placed his seatbelt on. Cordon didn't respond. "No problem then, because you'll end up right where you belong."

"His father probably a criminal too," The other said driving down the street.

"You probably right, man. He's going to be just like him."

Cordon was brewing inside but he wouldn't let them know. The only thing on his mind was Miranda and getting a hold of his father. He would leave them to their thoughts and opinions about him. They made it sound like his father was trash. Or a monster. They couldn't bother him anyway. But he couldn't explain why he was crying.

"We waited long enough, Leroy," Valencia whispered as they stood in front of the door. "You gonna give the nigga enough time to get better if we don't do it now."

"Shut up, bitch,'' he yelled in her face, "I got this!

Valencia was so nervous he was going to back out, that she was about to slap all the shit out of him and snatch the gun to ensure her plan would work. "Well it sure looks like you're scared to me. And a scared nigga don't make moves."

Taking blow after blow to his ego, Leroy decided to push off. He snatched the door open and walked out with the gun aimed toward the living room. The faint smell of Tech's rotten flesh was starting to permeate throughout the house.

Valencia walked behind him with her hands on his shoulders. "You see him yet?" she whispered into his ear. Her breath a little tart from not being able to brush her teeth in almost three days.

"No, but if you don't shut the fuck up, I'm about to punch you in the stomach," Leroy told her looking over his shoulder.

When they finally made it into the living room, Maine was sitting on the sofa, drinking a soda. One hand was between his legs. His eyes widened when he saw Leroy pointing the gun at him. "What's going on?" he asked with a frown.

"You tell me," Leroy said with the gun pointed at him.

"Why you got that shit in my direction?" he stared at the gun, "you cocked, too ain't you?"

"I'm sorry about this, Maine. I really am. But I'm gonna have to end our assembly right now. I hope you can understand. But if you don't, I guess I don't give a fuck either."

"Nigga, what the fuck are you talking about?" Maine said annoyed. "Please don't tell me you letting this bitch sing in your ear," he pointed at Valencia.

"It ain't about her," Leroy lied. "It's about me and my son. Something tells me that some lies were put out there about me and I'm not feeling staying here any longer. It's like it ain't safe."

Maine shook his head. "You the dumbest nigga ever," he paused. "Why are you listening to this bitch? She gonna get you killed."

"Don't try to put me in this shit!" Valencia jumped to her own rescue. "You dead meat. Deal with it! Okay?!"

"Bitch, even if he get out of here, you need to know that Flex not letting you go nowhere."

"Flex ain't got to let me do shit, cause me and Leroy rolling out now," Valencia rubbed his shoulders like it was the *Tree Of Hope* at the Apollo. "Ain't I right, Leroy?"

Silence.

"Leroy, listen to me," Maine placed his soda down, stood up and raised his hands. "This don't have to be like this between us. You hear what I'm saying?" he looked behind him at Tech's body on the floor. "She done already got one nigga killed. Are you in the mood to be the next?"

"I don't…"

"Fuck this shit," Maine said charging him. "I'm going for mines!"

Seeing three hundred and something pounds charging toward them, Valencia got out of the way.

Leroy tried to discharge the weapon but Maine was already on him like a warm blanket. Maine knocked him to the floor and stole him in the face multiple times.

"I told you that you were a dumb ass nigga! Didn't I?" *Left blow to the face.* "You let this bitch get you hemmed up for nothing and now you gotta take this ass whooping." *Right blow to the face.* "I didn't even feel like doing this shit." *Blow to the stomach.* "My shit hurt and it feels like somebody kicked me in the head." *Second blow to the stomach.* "But this the only thing you know."

Maine was treating him like his personal punching bag. He was about to snap Leroy's neck until he felt a stinging sensation in the back of his head and then his neck. To be sure he was really gone, Valencia started poking him like a raw steak.

Valencia stabbed him over and over until her elbow locked on her. She was panting heavily until she saw the gun to the left of them, she went for it but Leroy's pink wristed ass grabbed it first.

"Let me get that up off you," Leroy said in full possession of the firearm. He pushed Maine's body off of him and stood up. "Thanks for saving my life, baby girl. I owe you."

With an attitude she responded, "You welcome."

"I can't believe this nigga was about to kill me," Leroy said as he kicked Maine's body. "Punk ass mothafucka!" He looked at Tech's body. "It's sad what happened to your boyfriend, too."

Valencia looked at Tech. She was over his demise already. Although she loved him, there was nothing more important than distancing herself from Flex and his crazed father.

"May he rest in peace," she mumbled. "Well anyway," she sighed, "What's the plan now? Are you going your way and I'm going mine?"

He frowned. "That was never the plan and you know it," Leroy walked up to her. "You and I are officially joined at the hip," he grabbed Tech's car keys out of Maine's pocket. "So let's get out of here."

Valencia sat in the passenger seat of Tech's car. She was some kind of mad. She could smell Tech's scent and she suddenly missed him. Her life was a pile of wet trash and she wanted to change things. The only problem was, she had no idea where to start.

"What kind of person is Flex?" Valencia asked Leroy.

He sighed. "He's a good kid." He looked at her. "Why you ask?"

She pulled up her shoulders and dropped them back down. "Just asking I guess."

"He's about family. Does a lot for the people in his life. But," he continued to steer the car, "he has a darker side too. He's a killer. Got it from my father who killed first and spent time talking to folks graves later."

"If you know that, why did you rape his wife?"

Leroy shook his head. "Not that it matters, but I was high. She came over to drop off my grandson, and I was tweaking on heroin. Had been for most of the day. When I did that shit to her, she wasn't my daughter-in-law. She was just some woman. Any woman," he moved around a little in the driver's seat. "I ain't never been the best man in the world, but I sure ain't no rapist."

Valencia would beg to differ. Everything he just said sounded like rape to her. "So why didn't you just tell Flex what happened? And that you were high?"

"You sound stupid."

"I'm serious," she continued, "maybe if you told him you were on drugs, he wouldn't be so conflicted right now and kidnapping people."

"Me getting with his wife ain't got shit to do with his son going missing. I hate when people try to mix shit together."

"I'm not saying that," Valencia said. "What I'm saying is that he probably would not have been so mad at you if you were man enough to tell the truth," she exhaled and looked into the night. "I'm just thinking out loud I guess. Don't mind me."

"Well your thinking out loud ain't helping me none over here. Keep your dumb thoughts to yourself."

Valencia looked at him with disgust. "My bad," she rested her head back in the seat. "So where you taking me?"

"I figured to a hotel room," Leroy announced.

Her skin crawled.

"That way we can find out what we're going to do next."

"Happy, happy, joy, joy," she said clapping her hands.

"You know you got a real smart mouth. Anybody ever told you that shit before?"

She thought about Quita and Kimi. "A lot of people told me about my mouth, but I do and say what I want anyway."

"Tell me something I don't know already," he replied.

She rolled her eyes.

"Is that why Kimi called you and cursed you out?" Leroy questioned her. "Because of your mouth?"

"Kimi called and did that dumb shit because it's in her blood to be evil. Plus she puts me in a position of blame when it comes to her and Quita. She's done that since I've known her."

"Why is that?"

"Kimi thinks I used Quita to do the things I wanted. Like watch my twins and shit like that," she huffed. "But Quita is a grown woman who makes her own decisions. I don't have shit to do with that."

"Quita seems like a good person," Leroy speculated. "I saw in her eyes that she really cares about my grandson, and that might be the thing that saves her life." He got on the highway. "Where my son is concerned anyway."

"Quita may look like an angel but she's not," Valencia said in full hater mode. "And I wish people stop thinking that. Everybody in the world has flaws and that includes her fat ass."

"You seem bitter."

She leaned back and frowned. "Why the fuck I gotta seem bitter?" Valencia rolled her eyes at him. "Just because I made a comment about Quita? Give me a break."

"Not saying that's the reason," Leroy shrugged. "I'm just giving you my opinion about how you carry yourself."

"What you detect is not bitterness. Trust me. It's just that for as long as I've known Quita, she's always appeared to some like an angel. Not only that, she's famous for jocking my style. Bitches like that put a bad taste in my mouth."

He laughed. "What do you mean jocking your style?"

"For starters she moved into my house just to be near me. And when I asked her to watch my kids since she had a daycare center anyway, she started acting like my kids were hers. Trying to replace me by being their mother," she laughed. "I can't deal with no shit like that."

He looked over at her. "You're trouble."

"To some I'm trouble, to others I'm just me."

Valencia continued to think about her life. A scary thought entered her mind. Was it possible that she actually was the hater instead of everybody else? When she considered it hard, she decided it wasn't true.

Her mind was still on herself when she felt the car turning around. "Where you going?"

"I'm turning around," Leroy advised.

Her eyebrows stretched up. "What do you mean?"

"I can't do this shit. It's wrong."

"Okay, what is wrong? The fact that you raped your son's wife or the fact that you about to get both of us killed? Because it sounds to me like you're thinking about doing something real stupid."

Leroy bit his lip with the teeth he had left in his face. "I can't leave without talking to my son first. And apologizing for what I did," he looked over at her. "And I'm sorry, baby girl, but I'm going to have to use your life as leverage."

"Fuck!" she screamed out.

The van ride to the motel had Quita on edge. Instead of Clarkita sitting in the passenger seat like she had been all day, a deranged and angry father, took her place. At least Clarkita was in the van with her, while Essence stayed back to watch the kids.

"How come you don't have a license to watch kids?" Flex asked Quita out of the blue as they cruised down the street. "I never asked you that before."

"I had one, but it was revoked," Quita cleared her throat and continued to captain her vehicle.

"Why was it revoked?" he frowned.

She sighed. "When I first got my license, it was in Kimi's name. And since I was using Valencia's house, she also had to be in good standing."

He shook his head. "So she wasn't in good standing?" Flex asked.

Quita shook her head. "She couldn't stay clean. She smoked a lot of weed and since someone lied, and said we weren't taking care of the kids, our license was revoked."

"I'm not surprised. That classless bitch Valencia shouldn't be allowed near anyone's kids," Flex looked over Quita. "So what's your story?"

Quita looked through the rearview mirror. Although Clarkita knew her license was revoked, and still trusted her with her baby, she didn't know the history. "I have a record."

"I figured as much," he pushed. "But why?"

"For attempted robbery," Quita said in a throaty tone. "It was a long time ago though. I guess history can never be erased."

Flex leaned up against the door, eyed Quita and laughed. "What the fuck?" He pointed at her. "You robbed somebody? And got arrested? Just when I thought I heard it all, here you go."

"Yes I did it," she said insulted at his response.

"Who the fuck did you rob?" Flex was laughing so hard he couldn't contain himself. "I gotta hear this shit."

" I robbed a p…pre…" she said under her breath

He leaned closer. "What did you say?"

"I helped some dudes in the YBM rob a pastor," her skin was inflamed due to her embarrassment. "Of a church." Quita was so ashamed she wanted to cry. "He was dropping off a deposit from Sunday service and I helped them rob him. But instead of just taking his money, they beat him, too."

"So you were with the robbery without knowing who the mark was?" Flex shook his head. "Some people shouldn't leave their day jobs."

"It was dumb and I'm not proud of it," Quita continued. "I needed money for my mother's health care bills. So I was willing to do anything at the time. But the beat down, I didn't sign up for."

"YBM," Flex said scratching his head. "That's the YOUNG BLACK MILLIONAIRES gang right?"

"Yes," she rolled her eyes. "That's them."

Flex shook his head. "Them some dirty niggas if ever there was some," he looked out of the window. "I'm a monster, but even I have my limits."

Silence.

"Tell him the rest," Clarkita said under her voice. "You didn't finish your story."

Quita looked at her through the rearview mirror. "What are you talking about?"

"You can't just give him one part of the story, give him the rest, too," Clarkita clarified. "Tell him what happened after you robbed the pastor."

Quita was stunned. She didn't know Clarkita was up on her story. "I turned myself in, and took the blame. Because I wasn't willing to give up their names, they gave me some time. But the preacher forgave me, and verified that I wasn't involved with the battery."

Flex fell back into the seat, "So you ate a robbery charge?"

She nodded. "I couldn't live with myself either way."

Silence.

"That could not have been me," Flex admitted. "I'm not talking about the snitching part. That's the code of the streets. I'm talking about turning myself in. You could've paid him back by donating to his church or something."

"I guess we're different," Quita told him. "How did you know about the robbery, Clarkita? I never told you that before."

"I told you awhile back that I always know about everybody's background who might be involved in my baby's life. I thought what you did was honorable, so I forgave you."

Quita was blown away.

When they pulled up to the run down motel, Quita parked. "I don't know which room she was in," she looked at Flex. "You want me to go to the office or something?"

Flex was shaken up because he didn't respond. She could tell by how his body stiffened as he observed the motel that he was both nervous and hopeful that his son would be inside of the dwelling somewhere.

"No, I'll go inside myself," he pushed the van's door open and moved to the motel.

From the van Quita could see him going to room after room, knocking on each door. Some people opened windows and shook their heads that his son was not with them, and others came out and stepped to him with an attitude, until they saw the gun in his hand. Quita was counting down the time until someone went off on him.

"You think he gonna find him?" Quita asked Clarkita who always seemed to have an answer.

"I have a feeling we'll find something out, the question is what and when."

Two hours later, Flex stomped back to the van with an attitude. "I knocked on every fucking door in that bitch," he yelled pointing at the motel. "And don't nobody know where my son is at. How the fuck a kid just disappear off the face of the motel, and don't nobody know shit? Huh?"

"I think we should hang around here for a little while," Quita said calmly. "I got a feeling that this is the best place to be right now."

Flex's phone rang and he answered. "Hello," pause. "Celina, I can't do that right now," pause. "Why didn't you tell me grandma said she needed some money?" pause. "Okay, I'll be over in twenty minutes," pause. "I said I'm coming, Celina," Flex frowned. "But I gotta go now," he put his phone back in his pocket and looked at Quita. "I need you to take me to my sister's house."

"Okay," she replied shaking her head. "Although I really think we should stay right here." She pulled into traffic, "and where we going after that?"

"You gonna take me to that slut Pooh's house. I want her to answer for what she did to my kid."

Quita pulled up to a green house with a lot of toys in the yard. She eased her van behind a black sedan and parked. "We'll wait out here for you, Flex."

"I don't think so," he said opening the van door. "Both of ya'll coming with me. That way I can keep an eye on you."

"I been in and out of your sight all day, and never called the police or ran," Quita reminded him. "And now you gonna act like you don't trust me?"

"Both of you get out," he looked back at Clarkita. "Now!"

Quita rolled her eyes and they both jumped out of the van. The moment Flex opened the gate leading to the house, Quita could hear loud noises inside. They followed him up the front steps and he kicked a ball to the right, sending it flying into a basket ball hoop that was lying sideways in the grass.

From the outside it sounded like a bunch of kids were at an amusement park. Flex banged on the door loudly, five times, but no one would open it. When he didn't get an answer, he moved to the window and banged on it for a while, but still no answer.

When Flex walked back up to the door and kicked it with his foot, a lady with flour all over her face and in a black nightgown finally came to the door.

"I'm sorry, Flex, I didn't hear you knocking," she opened the door wider. Inside her home it looked like a junky toy yard and everything was out of order. "Where's my baby? I haven't seen Cordon all week."

"He's not here," Flex said with an attitude as he walked deeper inside, sending a doll baby flying to the corner after kicking it. "These are my peoples," he said looking back at them.

The moment Quita stepped into the threshold; a child smacked her in the face with something wet and red. When she jumped back and looked at it on the floor, she saw it was a bloody sanitary napkin that had been soaked with what appeared to be water.

"Rocky!" the woman yelled. "Why would you do that?"

The woman went about the business of chasing the rocky head three year old who was wearing a soggy pamper. When she finally caught him, she slapped him on the shoulder sending him running to the back of the house.

The woman approached Quita who was still staring at the nasty pad.

"I'm sorry," she said picking up the pad. Both Quita and Clarkita backed up. "He has a habit of picking up stuff from the bathroom trash, dunking it in the toilet and throwing it at people," she extended her other hand for them to shake. "I'm Celina. And you are?"

Quita and Clarkita looked at her hand and said, "With him."

She put her hand down. "Well you can have a seat if you want," She knocked a rack of toys off of some square thing that eventually revealed a couch.

Quita and Clarkita sat down knee-to-knee, afraid to touch anything else.

"Come on, Celina. I got to give you this money and get back out in them streets. I got shit to do."

"Okay, boy. Come on," Both of them disappeared into the back.

"What the fuck was that?" Quita asked Clarkita rubbing her face.

"I'm just as shocked as you are," Clarkita said relieved she didn't come into the house first.

While they were waiting on Flex, a five year old with knotty hair came out holding a very neat child's hand. The five year old immediately went up to Quita and started rubbing her knee. When Quita frowned, his light skin turned red. She was so scared that she popped up and moved to the other side of the living room. The moment she got up, the kid sniffed her seat and grinned again.

"I got to get out of here," Quita said shaking. "I ain't never in my life seen no shit like that."

"Sorry about that," the neat child said. He wore a black sweater over his blue dress shirt and red tie. "My name's Vickson and that is my brother Samson," he shook Clarkita's hand and then walked over to Quita to shake hers. "He's a little odd, but he's okay," the neat kid observed Clarkita. "Do you know my uncle Flex?"

"Yes," Quita smiled liking the kid immediately.

"He's a cool dude."

Neither Quita nor Clarkita chose to disagree although they had their own opinions. And none of them were good. "Can I get you something to drink?"

"We're both fine," Clarkita grinned. "You're a pleasant young man."

"I try," he said with lowered eyes.

When Samson started rubbing Clarkita's knee, she hopped up like Quita had. The moment she did, he sniffed her seat too.

"He just rubs your knee to get you to stand up. So he can sniff your seat," he nodded at his baby brother. "If you ignore him he'll stop."

Neither of them wanted to be molested by a kid so they remained standing. Five minutes later, Flex came out into the living room. The moment he looked at Vickson he said, "Where is it, man?"

Vickson frowned and backed away from him. "What are you talking about?"

Flex held his hand out, "Hand it over."

Vickson stuffed his hand into his jeans and handed Flex Clarkita's money clip.

"Oh my, God!" she pat her pockets. "How did he get that?" she took it from Flex.

"Too easily," Flex looked at them both. "Let's go. We got other shit to do."

Quita and Clarkita moved so quickly toward the door, they knocked over two of the children in the process.

"Bye!" all of them said waving at Quita.

Please God, if you give me nothing else in life, please don't let me see them kids again.

The moment Theresa opened the door, with a bandage around her arm, Flex knocked her to the ground by shoving her forcefully. He stepped over Theresa like he owned the place.

"Wait a minute, mothafucka!" she screamed from the floor. "Who are you and what do you want?" she rushed to the living room table and lifted her gun.

Theresa was about to shoot Flex when Clarkita held her back by holding the bandaged arm, "Don't do this shit now! Please!"

Theresa shook Clarkita off but not before Flex wrestled her gun out of her good hand. "Get the fuck off of me," she yelled in Clarkita's face. Clarkita released her hold. "Them niggas shot me in my hand and you grabbing my arm," she looked at Quita. "What is going on, Quita? Why are these niggas in my house?"

Flex was on a Pooh hunt as he rushed toward the back of the house. When he came upon a closed door, he kicked it open.

Pooh jumped up off the bed and started crying. "Please don't hurt me!" she dropped on her knees. "I didn't know what Kimi was doing! I didn't know. She never said shit to me!"

Flex ran up to her. "Where is my son?" he grabbed her hair so hard, he'd already yanked a pile of it from the roots "Because he ain't at the motel."

Quita and Clarkita walked into the doorway. "Pooh, just tell him anything else you know about Cordon so we can leave," Quita advised.

Pooh looked at Quita and then at Flex and fainted.

"I just need one more glass of water," Pooh told them sitting on the edge of her bed. Quita gave her another glass and she sucked it down like she didn't have a thing to drink all day.

Flex snatched the glass from her and handed it to Quita. "That's enough of the dumb shit," he stood in front of her. "Now tell me why you had my boy?"

"Okay, okay," Pooh doubled up on her words, "Kimi told me she needed me to watch Cordon because she had some place to be. She said she was watching him for Quita," Pooh looked at her.

"I didn't know anything about this," Quita said standing behind Flex. "If I would've known I would not have condoned any of it. So Kimi lied to you."

Clarkita shook her head at the entire situation.

Theresa hung in the doorway. And since Flex held on to her weapon, she hoped the meeting ended in her daughter's favor.

"I didn't think you knew Kimi had Cordon," Pooh said softly. "But I love my cousin and did what she asked me to do."

"Then why the fuck did you take him?" Flex frowned. "It seems to me that you got yourself twisted into something that didn't have to be. Are you dumb or something? If somebody told you to run into a hail of bullets, would you do it?"

"My daughter's many things, but she's not dumb," Theresa added her two cents.

Flex ignored her and focused back on Pooh. "Why did you do it?"

"I needed the money. Plus earlier that day Quita fired me for driving the kids without a license," Pooh paused and looked at Quita. "Anyway, when she first got Cordon, he seemed kind of sad. Kimi didn't like to see him that way so she gave me Vonzella's number to pick up her daughter Miranda. He likes her a lot, always has," she rubbed her hands together. "I was just doing what she told me," she looked into Flex's eyes. "That's all."

When Pooh paused Flex grew more irritated. "And what else happened when you had my son?"

"Kimi gave us some money for a cheap motel and we went there. I didn't understand why she told me not to answer my phone for anybody but her. And I didn't understand why she was acting so secretive. I'd been around Cordon a lot, and it didn't make sense to me. Until I saw his eyes. I never focused on them, until we were at the motel. He's her son right?" Pooh asked Flex.

"Why did Cordon leave?" Flex ignored her.

"Because Miranda was thirsty," Pooh hunched over. "He said he had money and they walked outside to get a soda. I waited for them to come back but they never came."

"What would make them up and leave the motel?"

"Maybe they were snatched," Pooh said causing everyone in the room to gasp.

"Don't say that shit again," Flex told Pooh pointing in her face. "Don't tell me somebody got my kid because I don't feel it in here," he placed his hand over his chest. "Now what else happened in that room? You holding back I can feel it."

Pooh sighed. "I don't know. I was talking on the phone to my boyfriend and Miranda kept staring at me."

"And?" Flex said feeling that she was leading somewhere.

"I think I was saying that Cordon looked like Kimi to Davie," Pooh bit her nail. "And that I had a feeling something bad would happen to Cordon and Miranda because Kimi didn't tell me she had a son." she looked at the ceiling. "And I may have said something about if Kimi kidnap these kids, that I don't want to be involved. I really can't remember."

"She was struck on the back of the head earlier today," Theresa told Flex. "Her mind may not be all together but she's telling you all she knows."

Flex looked at Theresa, "Shut the fuck up, bitch. I'm talking to her," he focused back on Pooh. "Now this shit makes sense." he shook his head. "They were worried that something was going to happen to them and they took off," he rubbed his face. "Okay, tell me which motel room you were in. I'm going back there."

"514," Pooh looked at everyone in the room. "I really am sorry about this," she got up and handed him the room key.

Flex stood up. "I'm going there now but If I don't find my son, I'm holding you personally responsible."

"Now wait one mothafuckin' moment!" Theresa yelled. "My daughter ain't got no hand in all of this by herself. You better go see about that Kimi," she said clueless to the fact that Kimi was already dead. "Now you have to leave," Theresa placed her hand on Flex's shoulder and he stole her in the face.

Theresa was hit with a haymaker that caused her to snore.

"Mommy!" Pooh jumped up to help her.

Flex placed his hand on Pooh's shoulder. "Like I said, if my son not there when I get there, I will be back. And when I do, it ain't gonna be sweet. Understand me?"

Quita, Flex and Clarkita were in the van driving back to the motel. You could cut the tension in the air with a knife.

"You know you didn't have to hit her right?" Quita said steering the van. "You could tell the girl didn't know what was going on. Kimi lied to everybody."

Flex looked directly into her eyes. "If you knew what I *was* going to do to her, you would've kept your comment to yourself," he shook his head. "The only reason she's still alive is because she was the last person to see my son, and I might have more questions."

Quita kept her comments to herself as she continued to maneuver the van down the road. When they pulled up at the motel, and parked, she almost swallowed her throat when she saw someone.

"Oh my, God," Quita said placing her hand over her mouth. "I can't believe this shit!"

"What?" Clarkita said sitting up in her seat to see out the front window.

"There goes Miranda right there," Quita pointed at the child. Everyone hopped out to meet her.

Although they were all in motion, no one was quicker than Flex. He removed his jacket, walked behind her and placed it over the little girl's shoulders. Then he walked in front of her and stooped down. The moment he did, Miranda socked him in the eye and attempted to run until she heard Quita's voice.

"Miranda!" Quita yelled. "It's me, baby. Please don't run! We won't hurt you!"

Miranda stopped in place, turned around and ran up to Quita. Quita gripped her up and swung her around. It was the best feeling Quita had all day. She placed Miranda down and Flex and Clarkita approached the two.

"Miranda," Quita said placing Flex's coat back over her shoulders, "you have to tell us where Cordon is. We've been looking for you guys all day and couldn't find you."

Miranda was shaking so hard, words wouldn't exit her mouth. She was cold and scared.

Quita smoothed back the loose hair strands surrounding Miranda's face. She looked into the child's eyes. "Try not to be so scared, Miranda. We aren't going to hurt you," Quita looked at Flex. "Now tell us what happened to Cordon. Where is he?"

Flex feeling like things weren't moving fast enough got in front of the girl. She was immediately scared because she just struck him. Miranda didn't know if he was going to retaliate or what.

"Miranda, my name is Flex and I'm Cordon's father."

When Miranda heard that, her body completely relaxed. She smiled at him and he smiled back. "He talks about you all the time," she told him. "I finally get to meet you."

"That's right, honey. But I need your help now. Can you tell me where he is?"

Miranda nodded yes. "We…we…were…were…." Miranda was obviously very cold.

Flex looked at Quita and said, "Lets get her in the van. She's freezing."

Clarkita rushed to the van and opened the back door for Miranda. Flex put her in the seat and eased next to her. Quita and Clarkita got inside also and closed the door.

"Quita, turn the heat on," Flex ordered. She did. "Miranda, I know you're cold and scared, but I need your help right now. Can you tell me where Cordon is?"

She nodded. "Yes."

He smiled. "Good. Where is he?"

"We were at the store, and he was trying to get something for me to eat," Miranda coughed and covered her mouth. "Excuse me."

"Okay and what happened then?"

Miranda lowered her head. "I don't want to get him in trouble. Because he was doing it for me."

"Doing what?" Flex asked with raised eyebrows.

"Taking the candy and stuff. Without paying."

"Why would he take candy?" Flex asked no one in particular. "Cordon had money. I see to it before he leaves the house every time."

"We left our coats in Ms. Pooh's room," she swallowed. "We wanted to get a coke because I was thirsty."

"Why did you leave the motel? Instead of just getting the soda?" Flex continued.

Miranda looked at Quita. Flex was making her nervous again.

"It's okay, baby," Quita said. "Tell him why you left."

"We left because I asked him to," Miranda admitted. "Because I heard Ms. Pooh say that Kimi was his mother," she looked into his eyes. "And that we were kidnapped and that something might happen to us. Is it true? That Kimi is Cordon's mother?"

Flex hadn't planned on being called out about Kimi. Prior to this moment, he planned to never tell his son about his biological mother. But with the news that he was already aware, things changed.

"Where is Cordon now?" Flex asked ignoring her question.

"The police took him," she said softly. "Because he stole from the store." She begin to cry uncontrollably. "I'm so sorry Cordon's dad. I really am. I didn't know he was going to get in trouble. I can get the money for the stuff if you want me to. So he won't be in trouble no more. My mommy don't give me a lot of money, but if I ask her, she might do."

Flex immediately saw the love in her eyes for his son and he felt proud. Although Cordon was just a child, he knew first love when he saw it. He had the same thing for his wife.

"Don't worry about that, Miranda," Flex told her patting her legs. "He's going to be okay. You did good by telling us where he is. If anything you're a hero and I'm not mad at you."

"Neither am I," Quita added.

Flex couldn't help but feel a sense of pride for his boy. He raised him right and a slight ounce of guilt panged him suddenly. Maybe he was wrong for denying Kimi access to her only son.

"Which store were you in?" Flex continued.

"I can show you," Miranda coughed and looked out of the front window. "Ms. Quita, you gotta go that way," she pointed. "I'll tell you where to stop."

After they arrived to the store where Cordon was arrested, and finding out which precinct he was sent to, Quita pulled in front of the station and parked. She felt like a taxi driver all day and was hopeful that her ordeal would soon come to an end.

"Quita, let me holla at you for a minute," Flex told her. "In private," he unlocked the van and slid out.

Quita hopped out too and stood next to Flex. "What's up? We're here so all you gotta do is go in and get him. Right?"

"That's what I want to talk to you about," Flex whispered. "I can't go inside."

She frowned. "Why not? You his father."

"Because I don't know if I have warrants on me or not," Flex told her seriously. "As a matter of fact, I'm sure I have warrants. If I go in there, they may run me and I'ma get locked up. So I need you to go inside and bring my boy back to me."

Quita paced in place. "But I'm not his mother," she threw her arms up in the air. "They won't just hand him over to me!" frustration caused her to lose it. "You gotta get him yourself, Flex. I've done everything you asked me to up to this moment. You took my mother! And since you won't tell me the status of Kimi, I know you killed her, too. And then you got my other friend tied up in her boyfriend's house. I'm tired, Flex and I'm not doing anything else!"

Flex scowled and snatched her by the arm. "Bitch, don't tell me what you gonna do and what you not gonna do. When I first met you at the daycare center, I told you what would happen if my son wasn't taken care of. You better be glad you still a part of this life and not the next," he continued. "Now until I have my boy in my arms, you haven't done shit but make me mad. This shit is all your fault anyway."

She pointed at herself. "My fault? How you figure?"

"Because you brought Kimi in the picture," Flex reminded Quita. "So as far as I'm concerned, you vouched for her."

"And you stole her child," Quita reminded him. "Let's not forget your part in all of this."

Silence.

"All I know is that it's almost the complete second day, and I still don't have my son. So are you gonna go in there and get him, or do I have to make you?"

Quita took a deep breath. Her hands were tied. "I'll see what I can do. But what if it doesn't work?"

Flex looked at the van. "It's a shame, I've taken a liking to Clarkita and Miranda," he focused back on Quita. "But if you don't bring Cordon, I won't hesitate to kill them both."

"You really are a monster," Quita said in a breathy tone.

"Call me what you want. But you better do what I tell you."

She sighed. "After I get Cordon, I don't want to have anything else to do with you for the rest of my life."

"Point taken," he paused, "now go get my boy."

****

Quita approached the police counter slowly. She swore everyone near her could hear her heart thumping. When she reached the officer she said, "I'm…to…Cordon."

"What?" the officer leaned in trying to understand her broken speech. "Can you speak up? I don't understand."

Quita cleared her throat and spoke louder. "I said I'm here to pick up my son."

"Okay, what is his name?"

"Cordon White," she grinned. "My son's name is Cordon White."

"Okay," he scanned through some papers on his desk. "What was he brought in for?"

"Shoplifting. Although I believe there must be some sort of weird mistake," Quita smiled again. "He had money and he's not a thief. Not only that, he's a child and shouldn't be held in jail without talking to his parents."

"If I'm not mistaken, we tried to reach his parents. He didn't know or give us a correct number. And since he is a child, and doesn't have a cell, we had to contact the Department of Child Services. Oh," he paused, "and if I had a dollar for every time someone told me that his or her child was innocent, I would be a billionaire."

Quita pouted. "Well is he still here or not?"

The officer flipped a few pieces of paper and then moved to the computer. He looked at the screen, squinted and said, "Yes he is here."

Quita's heart danced and she looked behind her at the van. She smiled and everyone inside smiled back.

Facing the officer she asked, "So what can I do to get him out of here? It's been a long day."

The officer continued to look at the screen and suddenly, his disposition grew angry. He looked up at her and asked, "Who are you again?"

"What do you mean?" Quita readjusted herself. "I just said I'm his mother. Now can you stop fucking around and go get my son."

"When we brought him in earlier, we asked about his parents. If I recall he told us that his mother is dead. So either you are the thickest corpse I've ever seen in my life, or you're lying. Which one is it?"

Quita's mouth felt dry and she leaned against the counter for support. She'd come so close to ending everything and now she was pushed back again. When she looked behind herself, at the van again, this time she was sad.

From the van, Flex immediately picked up on the change in her mood and tapped the window with the gun, out of view of Clarkita and Miranda.

Quita turned around and took a few quick deep breaths. She could not see another person killed today, especially because of her. So she faced the officer and said, "I've had a long day, sir. A *very* long one. Now my son made a mistake earlier, when he decided to remove himself from my view. But he's a kid so it's to be expected."

"And that still doesn't mean you're his mother," the officer told Quita. "So who are you, really?"

"Like I said, I'm his mother," Quita repeated. "Sir, I don't know what he told you, but he definitely didn't say his mother was dead. I suggest you go back and ask him again, or bring your superior to me."

"I said..."

"I don't want to hear anything else you have to say! Now I asked for my son, and if you don't bring him to me, I'm going to sue you and everybody else in this fucking precinct! Because at the end of the day he is a child and should be allowed to see a parent."

"I'll speak to him first," the officer pointed at her with a pencil. "But if I find out that you are lying to me, you'll have bigger problems."

Cordon was sitting quietly in the waiting area. He missed his father more as the time went by and was starting to think that he'd never see him again. He was just about to close his eyes in the chair, in an effort to get some sleep, "when an officer walked inside.

"Son, you have someone here to see you," he walked up to him. "But I have some questions first."

Cordon smiled and stood up. "Who is it? My dad?"

"No it isn't," he said softly.

Cordon's shoulders fell down. "Well, who is it then?"

The officer stepped closer to him. "Son, where is your mother?"

"I told you she's..." Cordon stopped in mid sentence. He remembered what his father always told him. *'Son, before giving a response to any inquiry, consider the question.'*

Cordon wrecked his mind. Why would he ask about his mother, when he was sure he already told him she was dead? Could someone be there posing as his mother? And if so who could it be?

"Son, where is your mother?" the officer repeated again.

Cordon swallowed and said, "She should be at home. Why?"

The officer glared and folded his arms over his chest. "I thought you told me your mother was dead."

Hearing the officer's comment made his stomach churn. Not only because it meant that he remembered what he told him, but also because he missed his mother.

"Sir, I never told you my mother was dead," he lied. "When I got in trouble I said, when she finds out what I did, I will be dead."

"You think you're so smart don't you?" the officer grinned. "You think you have all the answers. I'm not worried though, you'll be back here before long. I'm sure of it."

Silence.

"Okay," the officer said dropping his arms at his sides, "if your mother is out there, describe her for me."

"Why I gotta do that?" Cordon scowled. "Just let me see my mother."

"You're not going anywhere unless you describe your mother to me," the officer said loudly. "Now what does she look like?"

Cordon's mind floated. Who could be out there posing as his mother? It could be his aunt Celina, but she could never get a babysitter for her children. It could be his grandmother or even one of Flex's friends. It took him a minute to guess who would be there.

"Son, describe your mother," the officer said louder. "Now!"

He swallowed. "She's a little fat. She probably has her hair pulled back and she always looks scared. Her name is Quita," he said in a low voice.

The officer shook his head and Cordon was afraid he was wrong. "You're good. So good that I'm sure we'll meet again."

Cordon smiled. "I'm not good. I just know my mother."

Quita stood outside waiting on the verdict. Would they release Cordon or not? When she saw the officer return, with a frown, she was worried until she saw Cordon behind him. Her heart leaped out of her chest. After all this time, something she did worked.

"Here is your court date," the officer handed a folded document to Quita. "He has to answer to the charges of shoplifting in juvenile court. I just need to check your driver's license." Quita handed it to him and he took it to the back before returning it to her possession. "Okay," he looked down at Cordon, "I guess you're free to go."

When Cordon came around the corner, he ran into Quita's arms. She hugged him tightly and for a second, felt like he was her son. It was the longest day in her life and finally it would be coming to an end.

"I've been looking everywhere for you, Cordon." She grabbed his hand. "Come on, there's somebody who wants to see you."

When Quita and Cordon walked out the station's door, Flex was standing outside of the van. When he saw his son, with a close fist he hit himself in the heart three times. Finally, almost two days later, Flex was laying eyes on his child.

Cordon ran into his arms and Flex lifted him up. Tears ran down Flex's face and he squeezed Cordon tighter than he knew. "Son, I've been looking everywhere for you. Don't ever do that to me again. Ever."

"I'm sorry, dad," Cordon cried. "I'm sorry I left without you knowing where I was."

"Don't you worry about that now, Cordon," he placed him down. "You're here with me now and I love you."

For ten minutes they embraced. When they were done Flex said, "Let's get back in the van, I think somebody wants to see you."

The moment Cordon crawled inside and saw Miranda he hugged her. When they separated Cordon said, "So I see you met my dad."

Miranda smiled and said, "Yes…and I like him, too. He gave me his coat."

Cordon grinned. "So where we going now, dad?"

"To take your friend to see her mother."

Suddenly Miranda wasn't smiling anymore, and everyone in the van took notice.

"You must love the idea of dying," Valencia said to Leroy as he lead them to their deaths. "Why else would you be doing this shit?" She adjusted in her seat.

"I don't have to explain anything else to you," he looked over at her. "I told you what I gotta do. Now either you sit tight and go with the flow, or I might not take you to my son to see what he wants to do. I'll just kill you myself."

"Do you even know where Flex is right now?" Valencia questioned. "Because the last thing I heard, he was trying to find his son."

"I'm getting sick of your mouth, you silly dumb bitch!" Leroy yelled. "Now shut the fuck up!"

"And if I don't?" Valencia said no longer willing to bite her tongue.

Leroy clicked the weapon that rested in his lap. "Then I'll shoot you in your thigh, so you'll stay alive long enough to feel the pain."

Valencia threw her weight back into her seat and looked of the window. She was through with Leroy's black ass. She had to get out of that car. She looked around. She was doing what she should have a long time ago, look for something to use as a weapon.

There was a loose key next to her foot. Perhaps if she picked it up and stabbed it in his neck, she could run for freedom. But when she looked at his thick fleshy throat, she knew the key wouldn't be sharp enough.

When Valencia looked in the back, she saw a bat on the back seat. She could pick it up and bust him right in the head. Her heart kicked up knowing right away what she could do with it. But how could she get her hands on it?

She was about to go for it until Leroy said, "If you pick up that bat, I'ma gonna kill you with it," he focused on the road. "Now sit the fuck back and calm yourself down. And don't make me ask you again."

Valencia slumped in her seat and crossed her arms over her breasts. Oh how she hated his black ass. When she spotted the red top of a can of air freshener under her feet, she decided to go for it.

While Leroy was driving, she quickly picked it up and sprayed it in his face. A smell of strawberries filled the car. Leroy tried to hit her but his vision was altered.

There was one problem. Valencia hadn't thought her plan through clearly because he released the steering wheel. And when he did, the car crashed into another car.

Their heads snapped forward before bouncing unto their headrests. Another car flew from the left and stabbed into the driver's side. The impact caused their heads to knock together rendering both of them unconscious.

CHAPTER TWENTY-SIX

Cordon and Miranda drank hot chocolate in Valencia's kitchen, while Vonzella stood over them watching attentively. Her daughter was home and unharmed and she couldn't believe her eyes.

Quita and Flex stood a few feet away from everyone else. In the living room. His goon Morton stood behind him. "So what are you going to do with us now?" Quita asked him.

Flex looked at his son again. "What should I do?" he faced her. "If I let you all go, it could come back and haunt me later. All my life I've been the man who tied up loose ends."

Flex looked at Clarkita who was holding her baby. He also observed Essence who was staring at them.

Earlier that day, Cruella picked up Zaboy and luckily for them, she didn't seem aware of his earlier state of inebriation.

"We aren't going to say anything, Flex," Quita told him. "I promise you," she pleaded. "Let us get some normalcy back in our lives. Let us go back to our families," she sighed and looked at her hands. "Well, let some of us get back to our families."

Flex looked her over. Quita tried to appear as harmless as possible. He called out to his son, "Cordon, how about you take Miranda downstairs and watch some TV. I want to talk to the adults for a minute."

"Okay," Cordon smiled still happy to be with him.

When they both disappeared downstairs Flex addressed the women who piled into the kitchen with him and Quita. "I need a reason why I shouldn't wrap up my loose edges, and kill all of you now. Can somebody help me with that?"

Quita tried to speak first. "Because I…"

"I'm not talking to you," he looked at Clarkita first who was still holding her baby. "You've seen everything I've done today, why should I let you live?"

"Because I don't give a fuck if you kill me or not," Clarkita told him directly. "And because I have cancer and my doctor predicts I won't live more than two years anyway," she never told anyone before today. "The last thing I want to do is waste my time snitching on you," she kissed baby Axel. "I have a little more life to live."

Quita's heart thumped. After everything they'd gone through, she had grown to love the woman.

Clarkita's response appeared to work with Flex because he moved to Vonzella who was already sobbing. "What about you?"

Vonzella's bruises were still visible from what Mike did to her. "I don't want to die," she shivered. "I just want to take care of my daughter. Please."

As much as Flex hated to admit it, the fact that his son was sweet on her daughter was the reason he would let her live. For her sake, she had better hope that didn't change.

"What about you?" he asked Essence.

"You should let me live because I could've called the cops earlier, when you all were out and I didn't. Because I could've left and not stayed by Quita's side when everything hit the fan, but I didn't. I can hold a secret, Flex. Or I can take it to my grave right now if you kill me. It's your choice."

Flex remained silent for five minutes before finally speaking. "Your lives are on loan. Which means, if I ever get an impression that I've made a mistake, I will come to reclaim your souls," he looked at all of them. "Now give me some time alone with Quita."

The crowd dispersed, "It's your responsibility to keep an eye on them at all times."

Quita looked at Vonzella who looked so scared, she was liable to tell somebody. She wasn't sure if Vonzella would be able to hold water or not. "I don't want to be responsible for anybody, Flex. Let me just worry about myself."

When Flex raised his weapon and aimed at Clarkita's head Quita pushed his hand down. "I got them," she said out of breath. "Don't hurt them. Please."

"Are you sure?" he asked before tucking his gun.

"I'm positive," she sighed.

"Good, and for this favor you owe me. Big time. I'll collect on my favor later. Trust me," he tapped his soldier on the shoulder and they moved for the daycare center to get Cordon.

6 MONTHS LATER

When Valencia opened her eyes, she wondered what time she would be seeing Tech later that day. The last thing she remembered was that they planned to kidnap Leroy for ransom and she was wondering if it were a bad idea. But when she turned her head to the left, someone she hadn't expected to see was in her room.

Flex's goon Morton hung in the doorway and Flex walked up to the bed. "They said you came to earlier today. But you probably don't remember do you?"

"No," Valencia shook her head. "I…I…"

"You're having a lot of memory loss," he said as if she were a good friend. "It happens to most people who've been in a coma for six months."

"A coma for six months?" she touched her head. "What happened?"

"Let's see," Flex sighed, "well for starters, you and your boyfriend kidnapped my father and held him for ransom. I thought you had my son and things got out of hand. Remember that?"

"No…I…don't remember anything," she responded as a tear rolled out of her eye.

"Well you did," Flex assured her. "Anyway things didn't go as planned and you and Leroy, killed one of my best men after you almost bit off his dick."

Valencia was starting to remember everything, but for now she would continue to fake amnesia. "I'm sorry, I think there's been some…"

"I'm not finished," he interrupted her by raising his hand. "You and Leroy decided to get into your dead boyfriend's car, and got into an accident, which resulted in Leroy, my father, being killed."

Valencia could tell he was angry and was trying to think of something she could say to make things better. She sat up straight in bed and said, "I'm sorry for your loss."

"Don't worry about it," he replied kindly. "You took care of something I was going to do myself. For that, I thank you."

She felt slightly better. Still, what did he want from her? "What do you want now?"

"I came to collect."

"Collect on what?"

"On your life," Flex nodded. "Because although I didn't fuck with my father, for what he'd done to my wife, you and that stupid ass nigga you rolled with thought you could take somebody away from me. For money. And I can't have that."

"You said you didn't care," Valencia sobbed. "You were going to do it anyway. So what difference does it make?"

"You didn't know that when you kidnapped him," Flex looked back at Morton. "Finish her off."

"Please don't!" Valencia tried to scream before Morton walked up to her, stuffed a pillow on her head and shot her in the face.

Quita was moving into her brand new home in Fort Washington Maryland. After six months of nightmares, Quita had to come to grips with the fact that her mother, Kimi and Valencia were all murdered. It was time to move on with her life.

Quita was placing yellow paint on the walls in her basement because tomorrow she would be reopening her illegal daycare center. Luckily for her, all of her clients wanted to reuse her services, despite her hiatus. Quita's remaining client list included Vonzella, Miranda's mother, Cruella, Zaboy's mother and Clarkita. She could use the money too because although she had saved up quite a nice nest egg, most of it went to moving into her house and buying furniture for her home and daycare center.

The scariest part about her day was the call she received from Flex. He called to say that it was time to make good on the favor and she had no idea what he wanted from her. She didn't have money or anything useful to him, so she thought.

When Quita's doorbell rang, she placed the paint roller in the pan. She wiped her hands on the back of her pants and walked upstairs to answer the door.

"Who is it?" she asked, not looking out of the peephole. When no one answered she opened the door. The moment she did, she was considering slamming it back closed.

"Hi, Quita," Celina said with her children standing in front of her. "Flex said he told you we would be coming. I hope I'm not too early."

Quita looked at the riff-raft before her. "I...don't...I mean...what's going on?"

"I knew he lied," Celina smiled wider. "Anyway, I just got a new job and I need you to take care of my kids for me. The thing is, my job requires me to be gone for weeks at a time."

Quita's eyes rolled over three year old Rocky, who threw a wet used sanitary napkin in her face when she first met him. Then she considered Samson, the five year old with knotty hair who kept rubbing her knee, just to make her get up so he could sniff her seat. Lastly she looked at the kid wearing the tie and slacks. Quita discovered he was nothing more than a well-dressed thief. She knew right there that she would be doing anything but watching them.

"I think there's been a mistake," Quita told Celina as politely as possible. "I don't have any more openings available."

"Flex said you'd say that," Celina responded. "And he also told me to remind you about the favor." she pushed the kids in Quita's house and said, "I'll be back when I can. Enjoy!"

CARTEL URBAN CINEMA
WWW.CARTELURBANCINEMA.COM

COMING SOON

They never wanted the power,
but they stepped to the throne
PRETTY
KINGS
T. STYLES
NATIONAL BEST SELLING AUTHOR OF RAUNCHY

NATIONAL BEST SELLING AUTHOR OF *RAUNCHY*

The Cartel Collection
Established in January 2008
We're growing stronger by the month!!!
www.thecartelpublications.com

Cartel Publications Order Form
Inmates ONLY get novels for $10.00 per book!

Titles		***Fee***
Shyt List	________	$15.00
Shyt List 2	________	$15.00
Pitbulls In A Skirt	________	$15.00
Pitbulls In A Skirt 2	________	$15.00
Pitbulls In A Skirt 3	________	$15.00
Victoria's Secret	________	$15.00
Poison	________	$15.00
Poison 2	________	$15.00
Hell Razor Honeys	________	$15.00
Hell Razor Honeys 2	________	$15.00
A Hustler's Son 2	________	$15.00
Black And Ugly As Ever	________	$15.00
Year of The Crack Mom	________	$15.00
The Face That Launched a Thousand Bullets	________	$15.00
The Unusual Suspects	________	$15.00
Miss Wayne & The Queens of DC	________	$15.00
Year of The Crack Mom	________	$15.00
Familia Divided	________	$15.00
Shyt List III	________	$15.00
Shyt List **IV**	________	$15.00
Raunchy	________	$15.00
Raunchy 2	________	$15.00
Raunchy 3	________	$15.00
Reversed	________	$15.00
Quita's Dayscare Center	________	$15.00
Quita's Dayscare Center 2	________	$15.00
Shyt List V	________	$15.00
Deadheads	________	$15.00

Please add $4.00 per book for shipping and handling.
The Cartel Publications * P.O. Box 486 * Owings Mills * MD * 21117

Name: ________________________

Address: ________________________

City/State: ________________________

Contact # & Email: ________________________

Please allow 5-7 business days for delivery. The Cartel is not responsible for prison orders rejected.